Yuletide Protector

JANE BLYTHE

Acknowledgments

I'd like to thank everyone who played a part in bringing this story to life. Particularly my mom who is always there to share her thoughts and opinions with me. My wonderful cover designer Amy who did an amazing job with this stunning cover. My fabulous editor Lisa for all the hard work she puts into polishing my work. My awesome team, Sophie, Robyn, and Clayr, without your help I'd never be able to run my street team. And my fantastic street team members who help share my books with every share, comment, and like!

And of course a big thank you to all of you, my readers! Without you I wouldn't be living my dreams of sharing the stories in my head with the world!

CHAPTER
One

September 1st
8:32 P.M.

She couldn't wait for fall.

Ashley Fallon was sick of summer. However it was September now and in just a few weeks fall would officially begin. Warm sweaters, woolen socks up to her knees, cups of steaming hot chocolate, crackling fireplaces, pumpkins, apple pies, and Halloween and all the other good stuff that came in the fall was just around the corner. Knowing that made enduring muggy summer days more bearable, especially when she had plans with friends.

As she stepped out of the restaurant with her takeout bag, she glanced at her watch. She was running late. She was having dinner with her best friend, and she was supposed to have been there at eight-thirty, but it was already after eight-thirty. She'd had errands to run after work, she'd thought she would have had plenty of time, but the line at the grocery store was long, and the cashier was so slow. Then the hairdresser was running behind time, and Ashley had to wait half an hour before it was her turn. Then traffic was terrible, and the restaurant was busy, and it was at least a fifteen-minute drive to Sawyer's house.

Sawyer was one of those super punctual people who was never late for anything. Traffic, other people, the weather, none of it seemed to affect him, he was always there not just on time but early. She was the opposite and Sawyer was always complaining that whenever they made plans she kept him waiting, and today was obviously not going to be any different.

She had some major damage control to do.

Balancing her purse on her arm, she managed to keep hold of the bag containing their dinner as her free hand searched around for her cell phone. Her fingers curled around it, and she pulled it out, hitting speed dial one.

"You're late," Sawyer said as soon as he answered.

"Sorry," Ashley said but couldn't hide a small smile. Nothing was better after a long day than hanging out with your best friend.

"Let me guess, you just walked out of the restaurant with dinner."

"Actually, I'm halfway back to the car." She giggled.

She could practically hear the eye-roll come down the phone line. "Well, get your pretty little butt in gear and hurry up, I'm starving."

"Pretty little butt," she echoed. "I didn't know you spent any time looking at my rear end."

Sawyer cleared his throat. "I don't, I just want you to get here."

Hmm, that was an odd response. She'd just been joking, she didn't really think Sawyer cared about her backside, and even if he did look occasionally, he was just a guy, and he hadn't gone on a date in a really long time. Besides, they were best friends, and she was just as guilty of checking Sawyer out as he was of checking her out. He worked out a lot, as a bodyguard it kind of went with the territory, and she could appreciate his ripped body without it going any further than that.

"I'm going as fast as I can," she promised, darting across the road in a break in the traffic.

"What movie do you want to watch tonight?" Sawyer asked, his voice back to normal, there was really no need to be embarrassed about checking her out, but he was such a gentleman. She loved that about him, it made him safe, and after a couple of bad relationships she really needed a safe place.

"I don't care, whatever you want," she said. She was tired and doubted she'd even make it through the movie. She would probably end up falling asleep on Sawyer's sofa and then crash in his spare bedroom.

"Oh no," Sawyer said. "Last time I picked the movie you complained for a month about it."

Ashley laughed out loud. That was true, and she always told Sawyer to choose the movie and then complained about his choices. "Okay, you narrow it down to five, and then I'll make the final decision once I—"

She broke off as someone grabbed hold of her and yanked her into the alley she had been walking past.

For a moment she froze.

Her brain couldn't process what was happening.

Everything felt surreal.

Like it wasn't really happening.

She was being dragged further back into the alley, away from the busy road and all the people who were out for dinner or a walk, away from help.

"Ashley? Ash? Are you still there?" Sawyer's voice echoed in her ear.

That was what she needed to snap her back to reality.

She had to do something, if she didn't, it would be too late. She would be dragged too far away to be able to scream for help. She was a twenty-four-year-old woman, the chances of her physically overpowering her attacker were pretty much zero.

"Sawyer, help, someone's—" That was all she got out before her phone was yanked from her hand and thrown against the wall. She knew because she heard the shattering thump as it connected.

All of a sudden it really dawned on her.

She was all alone in this.

Whatever *this* was.

She knew it wasn't good.

This man was going to rape her, or kill her, or both.

And she didn't think there was anything she could do about it.

"Help," she screamed at the top of her lungs, praying someone heard her.

"Uh, uh, uh," her attacker said, slamming her up against the wall.

Pain spiraled through her back and momentarily knocked the air from her lungs.

As she struggled to suck in a breath, the man wrapped something around her neck.

A chain.

Automatically her hands lifted to claw at it, but she couldn't dislodge it.

The man yanked it tighter, and she could no longer draw in enough oxygen to sufficiently fill her lungs. White dots danced at the edge of her vision, but he didn't tighten it enough to cut off her air supply completely.

He didn't want her dead yet.

He wanted more from her than just her life.

The man held his face close to hers, and she got her first good look at him. Small brown eyes, messy dark hair, a mole on his cheek.

That he didn't care that she had seen him meant only one thing.

She wasn't walking out of this alley alive.

Ashley knew what was coming even before his hand took hold of the hem of her knee-length white skirt and shoved it up.

She worked as a secretary at a private security firm, she knew self-defense, she knew what to do, she should have done more before now, but there was a difference between knowing in theory what to do and putting it into practice in real life.

Although she was struggling to breathe, she couldn't do nothing, she couldn't go down without a fight. Ashley lifted her knee and managed to ram it upward, connecting with her target, her attacker's groin.

He sucked in a breath, and she knew that she'd caused him some pain.

That was small satisfaction because the blow didn't seem to do anything more than annoy him, and he shoved her a couple of times back against the wall, enough to stun her and send the world spinning like a top around her.

By the time her head cleared, the man was throwing her down to the hard, concrete ground and straddling her.

The chain around her neck tightened.

Cutting off her air supply.

Her fingers clawed at the metal until her fingernails were a mangled, bloody mess but it didn't do any good.

The chain was too tight, and the man was too strong.

Ashley fought as hard as she could. She tried to kick him, she tried to throw him off her, but he was at least twice her size, and her body was already weakening from the lack of oxygen. Her movements became clumsy and uncoordinated. Her limbs grew heavy, as did her eyes, and her vision was graying. She was getting cold, and fear was settling over her.

She hadn't felt it earlier, everything had happened too quickly and she had been too busy trying to get away.

But now that she knew she was going to die she was terrified.

She was going to die.

Die.

She didn't want to die. She was only twenty-four. She still had her whole life ahead of her. She wanted to get married and have kids, she wanted to travel, and she'd never told anyone, but she secretly wanted to write and record her own song, she'd always loved singing, but she was too embarrassed to sing in front of anyone.

Now she wasn't going to get to do any of that.

"Thank you."

Those were the last words she heard before she dropped into unconsciousness.

~

9:12 P.M.

Sawyer had no idea if he turned his car's engine off.

As soon as he got here he wanted only one thing.

To see Ashley.

When she had broken off in the middle of a sentence, he had known something was wrong. He'd thought maybe a car had nearly hit her—she never paid proper attention when she crossed the street—or that she had tripped over something—she was so clumsy sometimes. He hadn't expected that someone was trying to abduct her or kill her.

But that's what she'd said.

Before the line went dead she'd screamed for help and said that someone had her.

His heart had practically stopped.

As he'd jumped in his car he'd dialed 911, he knew Ashley's favorite restaurant so he knew where she would be. And he knew where she would have parked her car because she hated parking and she always went somewhere quieter and walked further so she didn't have to worry about squeezing into a tight spot.

He'd told 911 where he thought she was and he prayed they had gotten there in time, but that was it, that was all he knew. He didn't know if someone had abducted Ashley, he didn't know if she had been murdered, he didn't know anything, and that was terrifying.

Sawyer scanned the scene.

There were two cop cars and an ambulance all parked in front of an alley, so that was where he headed. A cop was just rolling out tape and shot him a look that clearly said he was about to be told to move along.

He would *not* be moving along.

He was here to find Ashley and nothing and no one was going to stop him.

"I was the one who called 911, I was on the phone with Ashley when someone grabbed her. Is she alive?" The words came out in a rush as he preempted the cop telling him to get out of here.

The woman debated for a moment, then her face softened and her eyes filled with empathy.

Sawyer's heart almost stopped.

Was the sympathy because she was about to tell him Ashley was dead?

"She's over there," the cop said, lifting a hand to point to a stretcher that was being carried out of the alley.

He took off toward it then stopped dead in his tracks when he saw

Ashley's still form. There was a tube down her throat, and one of the paramedics was bagging her.

One of the medics caught sight of him. "She's alive. You the one who called it in?"

"Yes." Sawyer took a tentative step toward Ashley, scanning her for injuries. Her throat was bright red, and he could see marks indented in the skin of her throat in the shape of small ovals one beside the other, it looked like she had been strangled with a metal chain.

"She can breathe on her own, we were just concerned that her throat was going to swell closed as the bruising came out and decided we should be safe rather than sorry," the other medic explained.

Relief nearly knocked him off his feet.

Ashley was okay.

Alive.

He'd never been so scared in his life as he'd been these last thirty minutes. Ashley didn't know it, but he had been in love with her since they'd met three years ago. She was sweet and funny, kind and thought-ful, and drop-dead gorgeous, with long jet black hair and soulful brown eyes.

"Are you coming with us to the hospital?"

"Absolutely," he said as he climbed into the back of the ambulance behind the stretcher. As much as he was positive he didn't want to know, he had to ask, "Was she sexually assaulted?"

The medic who had stayed in the back with him averted his gaze but nodded. "They'll do an exam in the hospital, but from the looks of things, she was."

For a second Sawyer felt like he was going to be sick.

How was he going to tell Ashley that when she woke up?

That he was the one who would tell her was a forgone conclusion as far as he was concerned. Ashley was an only child whose parents had her later in life, they had both passed away not long after he met her. The cops could do it, but they would be too detached. It wasn't that they wouldn't care, but their job was to find the person who had hurt her, as her best friend, his job was to protect and support Ashley through this.

"Did they get the guy who did it?" he asked.

"No, I'm sorry." The medic finally met his gaze. "He must have run when he heard the sirens. You saved her life. If she hadn't been on the phone with you when he grabbed her, and you hadn't known where she was, then she wouldn't have survived. She had already passed out by the time the guy got spooked and ran. Another minute or two and she would have been dead."

Minutes.

Ashley's life had come down to a matter of minutes.

Sawyer couldn't help but shudder at the thought.

He reached out and picked up her hand, carefully avoiding the needle in the back, and tried to reassure himself that she was all right.

It didn't take long for them to reach the hospital and as he followed the paramedics inside, he spotted his sister and her husband. Savannah had reconciled with the man she loved last Christmas, and they had married in the spring. He loved seeing his twin so happy and content, and Sawyer's gaze dropped to Ashley's pale face. If the man who attacked her had succeeded in killing her then he would never get a chance to find out if there could be anything between them. He feared they were too firmly stuck in the friend zone, so he had tried to be content with that, but it was hard. Spending so much time around Ashley and never letting on how he really felt was like a form of torture.

"Sawyer." Savannah obviously spotted him, and with her husband's arm around her waist, she hobbled over. After being attacked twice by two different psychopaths, both times having the same hip shattered, Savannah walked with a limp. The injury had also ruined her dreams of becoming an FBI agent, so instead, she had joined the FBI's evidence response team. He wondered if he should ask her to go to the scene and see if she could find anything. It wasn't that he distrusted the crime scene unit it was just that he trusted his sister more.

"She's alive," his brother-in-law, Jett Crane, said when he and Savannah reached him.

It sounded more like a statement than a question, but he nodded anyway. "She was unconscious but still breathing when the cops and medics arrived. They intubated her because they were worried her airways might close as the swelling increases. Did you speak with anyone? Do you know anything?" he asked Jett. His brother-in-law was an FBI agent, and he was hoping Jett and his partner might find a way to help with the investigation.

"I don't need to speak with anyone. I already know more about the man they're looking for than they do," Jett said, his green eyes full of anger, empathy, and determination. "We don't know who he is, but he's raped and killed sixteen women in four states over the last three years. Ashley fits his preferred victim type, early to mid-twenties, dark hair, brown eyes, pretty. He grabs them in a reasonably public location, usually pulling them into an alley near a busy shopping or restaurant strip. He rapes them and then strangles them to death with a metal chain. As soon as I heard Ashley had been strangled and assaulted by a man with a metal chain, I knew it had to be this guy. Blake and I were assigned this case two and a half years ago, I've been trying to catch him ever since."

Sawyer didn't miss the darkness that crossed both Jett and Savannah's faces at the mention of Jett's ex-partner who had gone off the rails and embarked on a killing spree that almost got all three of them killed.

"Ashley is the only surviving victim," Jett told him. "If she saw his face then she could be the key to finally finding this guy."

She was lucky to be alive. It was only the fact that he had been on the phone with her when it happened that she had survived.

He could have lost her.

He had come within mere millimeters of it.

But he hadn't.

He hadn't lost her.

Ashley was alive, and hopefully, she knew something that would help Jett and Morgan catch this guy before he went after another innocent woman. Then the process of healing would begin. It would take her a while to recover, emotionally and psychologically more than physically, but he would be there for her every step of the way, whatever she needed he would give her.

"I'm going to go sit with her," he announced.

"We're here if you need anything," Savannah said, reaching up to kiss his cheek.

Sawyer appreciated that. "Maybe you could both go check out the scene."

"We will," Jett promised. "Morgan should already be there, I texted her as soon as I realized who it was. We'll find this guy, Sawyer."

He wanted to believe that, he really did, because he thought knowing the person who tried to kill her was in prison was the only thing that would give Ashley the peace of mind she needed to move on.

CHAPTER
Two

September 2nd
11:46 A.M.

"Hey, sweetheart."

Those were the first words she heard, and they reassured her more than the soft mattress she was lying on, the warmth, and the smells and sounds that all told her she was in a hospital. Knowing Sawyer was here with her made her feel safe, and Ashley had no doubt that he had saved her life.

She blinked open her eyes, and the first thing she saw was Sawyer's face. He was perched in a chair beside her bed, holding her hand, and she knew he had been sitting there since she was brought here.

She was alive.

Ashley had no idea how but she was so thankful, and she owed it all to Sawyer.

Tears filled her eyes and tumbled out when she blinked, but when she opened her mouth, Sawyer stopped her. "You can't talk, honey. When he strangled you, he damaged your throat. You'll have to keep quiet for a couple of days then your voice should be okay. I know that'll be hard for you," he teased, offering her a bright smile, but she could see the fear and concern lurking in his blue eyes.

Because she knew that he was worried, she forced her lips to curve into a smile for him.

"That's my girl," he said, a little of the anxiety disappearing. "You want some water to drink? The doctor said you can try a little, but if it hurts too much don't persist with drinking. You have an IV." He gestured to the needle in the back of the hand he wasn't holding. "So you don't have to drink, it's giving you the fluids you need. Do you want some water?"

Sawyer was rambling, he always did that when he was worried. Since it seemed like she was going to be okay, it wasn't her physical condition that was worrying him. It was probably because he was concerned that she was going to fall apart.

She wasn't.

Not yet anyway.

Ashley felt like she was in some sort of alternate zone.

She knew she had been attacked. She remembered being on the phone with Sawyer when she was dragged into the alley. She remembered the chain around her neck choking the life out of her.

She remembered all of that, and yet she felt removed from it.

Like it hadn't happened to her.

Like she had watched it happen to someone else.

Kind of like an out of body experience.

Ashley knew that it would hit her later. She knew that at some point she probably was going to fall apart, but not right now.

She nodded at the cup Sawyer held uncertainly in his hand, and he moved it over and held the straw to her lips.

It wasn't until the cool water touched her throat that the pain hit.

She winced and pushed the cup away.

"Did that hurt?" Sawyer asked. When she nodded, he asked, "Do you want me to get the doctor to give you some more painkillers?"

She shook her head, not ready for anyone else to come into the room, and there were questions she needed answers to. Since she couldn't speak she was going to have to ask another way. Ashley gently tugged her hand free from Sawyer's and made a writing motion.

"You want a pencil and paper?"

She nodded, this communicating with head nods and shakes was going to get old really quickly, hopefully her throat would be good enough for her to try talking sooner rather than later.

Sawyer ducked out of the room, and the sight of the door closing behind him and the realization she was now alone almost had her scrambling out of bed after him. If he hadn't returned in under a minute she probably would have. Ashley wasn't used to being afraid of being alone. She had never been one of those kids who was scared of the dark, she was the kid who loved horror movies, and who thought it was funny to hide and jump out and boo someone. She hoped this panicky feeling when she was by herself wasn't going to last long. It might be naïve of her, but she didn't want the attack to change her life or who she was.

"Here you go." Sawyer sat back beside her, and she felt herself settle.

She took the pencil and notebook that he held out and tried to decide what she wanted to ask first. There were so many questions running through her head, she supposed she might as well go with the most important. She wrote it down then turned the paper around so Sawyer could read it.

"How am I still alive?" he read aloud. "Because of good timing. When you told me that you needed help on the phone and then the call got disconnected, I dialed 911 and told them where I thought you were. Apparently, they arrived just in time. You were unconscious but still alive, another couple of minutes and..." he trailed off.

So she had been right. Sawyer was to thank for her being alive. He had saved her, he was forever going to be her hero. She pulled off that sheet of paper and wrote her next question.

"No, I'm sorry, Ash, the cops think he got spooked when he heard the sirens and ran. But I spoke with Jett, and he says he believes he knows who the man is. This guy has raped and killed sixteen women over the last three years."

Raped and killed sixteen women.

Raped and killed.

Raped.

Had she been raped?

She didn't remember that.

She remembered everything else, but she had no memory of that whatsoever.

"Ash?" Sawyer stood and moved to sit on the edge of the bed. Her eyes met his, and she saw his grow wide. "You didn't know he raped you," he said, dismay dripping from every word. "I'm so sorry, honey." He took her hand and squeezed it as though he could make everything better just by being there.

Funny thing was, it did help just to have him there.

He was her best friend and the closest thing she had to family since her parents had passed away a few years ago.

"I think you should close your eyes, get some rest," he said, smoothing her hair.

Part of her wanted to say no she was never going to sleep again, but the other part of her was exhausted.

Ashley was going to close her eyes when she thought of something. Sawyer said that the man who tried to kill her had already murdered sixteen other women and he was still out there. That meant that she was the only one who had seen him and lived to tell about it. Anything she could tell the cops could help them get him, and there was one thing he had done that seemed odd.

She quickly wrote down what she remembered then handed the pad to Sawyer.

He took it, read it, then said, "That's what he said to you? Thank you?"

She nodded, then reached out and added, 'Just before I passed out'.

"That's odd," he said thoughtfully, absently passing her the notepad back. Sawyer opened his mouth to say more, but the door opened, and a doctor walked in.

She couldn't help but tense. Her attacker was still out there, and she didn't want anyone she didn't know near her.

"I'll go wait outside while he checks you over, I'll call Jett and tell him what you told me. Be right back, okay?" He pressed a tender kiss to her forehead, then left.

Alone with the doctor, Ashley felt her whole body tense, she wanted

Sawyer back. She wanted a doctor she knew to look after her. When Sawyer came back she would ask him if he could call Brian Xander who worked as a doctor for the private security firm they both worked for.

It wasn't until the doctor stood beside her bed and pulled off his mask that she realized who it was.

Small brown eyes, messy dark hair, large mole on his cheek.

She knew him.

He wasn't a doctor, it was the man who had tried to kill her.

He must have figured out she was still alive, or maybe the press had reported that she had survived, but whatever the reason he had obviously come back to finish what he started earlier.

She opened her mouth to scream, but nothing came out except a hoarse croak, nothing that anyone would hear.

The look he gave her was almost apologetic like he regretted what he was about to do, but she knew he didn't. He had tracked her down here, either he was a doctor or he had stolen a set of scrubs and come to her room to kill her. He definitely wanted her dead.

His hands wrapped around her already aching throat and began to squeeze.

She wasn't going to die.

She wasn't.

Ashley already knew that fighting the man off wasn't going to work, it hadn't last time so why would it this time when she was weaker than she'd been before.

The only way she was going to survive was to play it smart, not strong.

She still held the pencil and pad in her hand, she could throw it at the door, but she doubted that even if it got there it would make much sound. So instead she aimed the pad at the glass of water on the small table beside her bed.

The man's hands around her neck tightened and her vision grayed. If she didn't do it now she would lose her only chance.

Ashley tossed the pad with all the strength she had and was rewarded by the sound of shattering glass.

She was just passing out when she heard the door slam open.

~

12:21 P.M.

Stepping out of Ashley's hospital room to give her some privacy as her doctor examined her, Sawyer closed the door behind him and pulled out his phone.

"Do you know anything yet?" Sawyer asked as soon as Jett answered the phone, it had been a while since he had called for another update, and he was hoping they had something, however small.

"No, I'm sorry, Sawyer, nothing yet, but we're all working this as hard as we can."

That wasn't what he wanted to hear.

This guy had been roaming the streets raping and killing for three years. How did they not even know who he was?

"Ash is awake," he told Jett. "You should come down and interview her, she can't speak yet, but first thing she did was ask for a pencil and paper so she could find out what happened. She told me something strange about the guy, apparently he thanked her."

"Thanked her?"

"She said, just before she passed out the last thing she remembered was him saying thank you. I know it's not something that's going to lead you straight to him, but—"

"But it will definitely help us with our profile," Jett finished. "Savannah and I are on our way to the hospital, if you want to take a break, Savannah will sit with Ashley for a while so she's not alone."

While he appreciated his sister's offer, he wasn't leaving this hospital until Ashley did. She needed him, and he was going to be there for her. "Thanks, but—" He broke off when he heard what sounded like shattering glass coming from Ashley's room. Had she tried to get out of bed and knocked something over? He wouldn't put it past her. "Jett, I have to go, something just fell over in Ash's room. I'll see you guys soon."

He shoved his cell phone back into his pocket and opened the door to Ashley's room. He expected to see his best friend trying to convince the doctor to let her go home, which was never going to happen. The doctor he'd spoken to in the emergency room had told him they'd be keeping Ashley here for a minimum of twenty-four-hours so they could monitor the swelling in her throat.

Instead, he found Ashley on the bed, the doctor's hands wrapped around her neck.

The second he heard the door opening the man's head snapped toward him.

Without hesitation the man ran, shoving into him and knocking him over as he bolted out the door.

He had to make a choice, go after the man—who he had no doubt was the same man who had tried to kill Ashley yesterday—or check to see if she was still alive. If she had stopped breathing and he delayed even a minute it could mean she wouldn't survive.

It was really no choice.

Sawyer ran to Ashley and pressed his fingertips to her neck, his other hand rested on her chest. Her pulse thumped beneath his fingers, and her chest rose and fell with each breath she took.

She was alive.

Satisfied that although she was unconscious she would be okay, he took off out the door. "Where did the doctor who just came out of Ashley's room go?" he demanded, pouncing on the nearest person, a nurse who he recognized had been checking on Ash throughout the night.

"He went down there." She pointed toward the elevators. "What's going on?"

"Call security, see if they can shut down the hospital, the killer was just here. And get a doctor in to check out Ashley, she's still breathing, but she's unconscious." He debated going after the man and trying to find him, he wanted to rip him to shreds with his bare hands, but that was exactly what he'd have to use. He didn't have his gun on him, he hadn't thought he'd need it here at the hospital. There was no way to know the killer would have come back to try to finish what he started.

A doctor went rushing past him into Ashley's room, obviously the nurse had done what he'd asked while he had stood there like an idiot trying to decide what he should do.

Attempting to find the man in the hospital would be like trying to find a needle in a haystack, it was probably best to stay here in case he doubled back. Was he really a doctor here or had he just dressed in a pair of scrubs and blended in to come after Ashley?

Sawyer paced agitatedly backward and forward outside Ashley's door like a sentry, which is exactly what he saw himself as. Whether she liked it or not, Ashley needed a bodyguard until this guy was caught. He had already made his intentions clear, he wanted Ashley dead, and he wasn't afraid to try to kill her in the middle of a busy hospital.

"Sawyer."

He turned at his name and saw Savannah and Jett coming toward him. "He was here."

"Who was?" Jett asked.

"The killer."

"What? When?"

"Just now. When I told you I heard something in Ash's room it must have been her trying to get my attention. When I went in, he had his hands around her neck, but he ran as soon as he saw me." The man was a coward. He picked on people physically smaller and weaker than himself and rather than take on someone his own size, he ran away.

"Is she okay?" Savannah asked.

"She's alive," he replied. That was really all he knew, the doctor hadn't come back out yet, so he hadn't been able to get an update. As if his thoughts propelled it into happening, the door behind them swung open, and the doctor came out. Sawyer pounced. "How is she?"

"She's awake and asking for you, I assume you're Sawyer."

"I am. She's all right?"

"Her throat didn't need more trauma after what it just went through. We'll need to observe her for a while longer to make sure her airways don't swell closed, but yes, physically she's as stable as she can be."

"Thank you." He nodded at the doctor, dismissing him. Then he turned to Jett. "I'm putting her in a safe-house until this is over. He wants her dead, and I don't think he's going to stop. This is the only time he's messed up, and he's not happy about it. He knows that she's seen his face, she can identify him, he can't let her live and he's made it clear that if he has any say in it she won't."

"I think that's smart." Jett nodded. "And I promise we're doing everything we can to find him, as soon as she's strong enough, we'll interview her to see what she knows, hopefully it's enough to at least point us in a direction."

"The doctor said she's awake, you may as well come and interview her now," he said. He knew Ashley and knew she wouldn't rest until she'd told the cops everything she knew.

Sawyer opened the door and found Ashley in the bed, the pad of paper in her hands writing furiously, and he couldn't help but smile. Ashley was amazing. She was so strong, and she was always going above and beyond. There had been many times that she had reached out to clients of the private security firm they both worked for to make sure they were okay, or to see if there was anything she could do to help them. She was always thinking about others and what she could do for them.

Even as she lay in a hospital bed, almost killed twice in less than twenty-four-hours instead of resting and recovering, she was trying to write down everything she could remember about what had happened to her and the man who had done it so they could hopefully catch him.

Her spirit reassured him, it was what was going to get her through this. "Hey, you. You should be sleeping."

She looked up with a small smile, relief in her dark eyes. He was glad to know that having him here made her feel better.

"Hi, Ashley." Savannah walked over and kissed Ashley's pale cheek.

"Is that for us?" Jett asked, gesturing at the paper in her hand.

Ashley nodded.

"It was the same man wasn't it?" Jett asked.

Ashley nodded again, then tore off the paper and handed it to Jett.

"Thank you for doing this," Jett told her, scanning the information she'd given him. "I'll send a sketch artist to work with you. It looks like you remember quite a lot about what he looks like, hopefully we can get a good sketch out there. If we can, we might be able to get someone who knows who he is to turn him in."

"Ash." Sawyer sat on the edge of the bed beside her and took her hand, she curled her fingers around his and held on tightly. "Until this guy is caught, I'm going to be your bodyguard, and you're going to come and stay with me. He wants you dead, he could come back again and again, we need to play things safe, and that means doing whatever's necessary to keep you alive."

He waited a little anxiously to see Ashley's reaction.

He had expected her to disagree, protest, and tell him—even if she couldn't use words—that she didn't need anyone to look after her.

But she did none of those.

Instead, tears welled up in her eyes, and her bottom lip trembled.

She had held it together amazingly well so far, but no one could go through what she had and not be affected.

Ashley hesitated for a moment and then she threw herself into his arms and sobbed into his chest.

Sawyer held her and wished with all his heart there was something he could do to take away her pain. He felt so helpless feeling her tears soak through his t-shirt, there wasn't anything he could do to make this better for her. All he could do was be here, and nothing would stop him from doing that.

CHAPTER
Three

December 21st
9:09 A.M.

Ashley sat in Sawyer's townhouse staring out the window.

She couldn't believe it had been well over three months since her life had changed forever.

The last few months had been surreal.

It felt like it had been forever, and yet at the same time, it was like she had blinked and it was Christmas time.

Christmas.

It didn't feel like it was Christmas, it hadn't snowed yet, and she needed snow to feel Christmassy. Ashley had always loved the snow, she had even done competitive skiing for a while. Even as a small child her attitude had been endure the warmer months to get back to winter. She loved watching snowflakes fluttering through the air, she loved the feel of them landing on her skin and leaving tingling cold dots everywhere they landed. She loved the crunch fresh snow made when you walked on it, she loved building snowmen and throwing snowballs, and snuggling up in front of a roaring open fireplace, sipping hot chocolate as the snow poured down outside.

No snow meant no Christmassy feeling, and she really needed something good in her life right about now.

For three and a half long months, she had been cooped up inside Sawyer's house. It wasn't that she wasn't grateful to him for making space in his home and his life for her. He had basically given up everything, but staying here with her day and night, and night and day. He thought it was too risky for her to go out very often, so although they took the occasional trip to the grocery store or went for the occasional jog, that was it. The rest of the time she just hung around in here. She was sure that Sawyer must be sick to death of the sight of her by now.

She'd had to give up everything, including her home. The private security firm she worked for was run by three ex-cops, Ryan Xander, Paige Hood, and Brady Crowley. In order to try and keep her safe, it had been reported to the media that she didn't survive the second attempt on her life which meant as far as anyone outside the small circle of cops and co-workers was concerned, she no longer existed. Brady's wife Aurora was a real estate agent and had arranged for it to look like her house had been put on the market following her death, and all her stuff had been boxed up, and other than the few belongings that had been brought to her here at Sawyer's, the rest of her belongings were being stored in her basement.

All of that made her feel so lost.

So alone.

It was weird being dead.

She couldn't really describe the feeling, and since she didn't know anyone else who had gone through what she was going through she didn't even have anyone to talk with about it.

Sawyer had been amazing. He was so supportive, worked so hard to cheer her up, and had been beside her every step of the way. Through every tear, through every angry outburst, he had just been there. She was never going to be able to thank him for everything he had done for her. She had really lucked out when she'd gotten him for a best friend.

The doorbell rang, but she didn't tense. The only people that ever came over were their friends, and besides, the killer was hardly going to ring the doorbell if he managed to find her here.

Ashley was starting to feel like all of this was a waste.

As far as the killer was concerned she had been reported dead, he had no reason to think she was a threat to him. This had to be over sooner or later.

It wasn't like she could live here like this forever.

At some point she was going to have to go back to her regular life. She wanted to so badly. She wanted to go back home, back to work, and back to her routine. She wanted to get her hair done and go out to eat at her favorite restaurants, and she wanted to go to the movies, and the gym, and just be a regular person.

"Hey, Ash."

She tore her eyes away from the gray world outside.

Gray.

It was the color of nothingness.

It was the color of her life.

It wasn't the color of Christmas.

The color of Christmas was white.

White was peace and love and purity, it was hope, it was all things good, it was clean and beautiful.

Just like Christmas was supposed to be.

But this year it was ruined, just like her life.

There had been lots of moments of self-pity the last few months, plenty of wallowing in the mess her life had become, and today seemed to be one of those days.

No.

She wasn't going to do that.

She was alive.

She had cheated death twice, that was something to be grateful for.

And whether it felt like it or not it was Christmas time, and Christmas time was a time for miracles, who knew, maybe this Christmas she would finally get her wish, and the man who had raped and tried to murder her would be found and caught. If she was still young enough to write a letter to Santa that would be the only thing on her list this year.

Deliberately, she forced her mouth to curve into a smile, she wasn't a spoilt brat—well, she had been spoiled as an only child, but she wasn't a brat—and she was a glass is half full kind of girl, so she should act like it.

"Hey." She turned and smiled at her friends. Samara Patrick was a friend she had met through Sawyer's sister Savannah. Samara was the younger sister of Savannah's best friend Chloe's husband. And Aurora was the wife of one of Ashley's bosses. She liked to hang out with both of them, and both of them had made sure to stop by at least a couple of times a week to see her. She really appreciated how amazing her support group had been, if it wasn't for them, she didn't know how she would have survived these last months.

"We brought wrapping paper, boxes, ribbons, and bows," Aurora announced, her golden-brown eyes glowing with delight. Ashley knew Aurora loved Christmas almost more than she did because it was Christmas Eve a few years back that she had met her now-husband Brady.

"We thought we could hang out, wrap a few Christmas gifts, start stacking presents under the tree," Samara added, her blue eyes serious, just like they always were. Ashley wasn't sure she had ever seen Samara look relaxed. They had fun together, but Samara was always quiet and solemn, Ashley always wondered what had happened to her to make her so sad.

"Wrapping gifts sounds like fun," she said, and pushed herself out of the rocking chair in the corner, and walked over to the kitchen table.

"I have to wrap on the floor," Aurora said, sitting down on the floorboards with a bag of presents and a roll of wrapping paper.

"Did Brady come with you? Are he and Sawyer talking?" Ashley asked as she grabbed her own bag of presents and took them over to the table. Since she hadn't been able to go out to the mall to do her gift buying this year she had purchased everything online.

"Yeah they're in the living room talking," Aurora replied.

About her no doubt.

She knew they were all worried about her. Sawyer's brother-in-law Jett and his partner Morgan had been working this case every single second they could, but so far they still didn't even know the name of the man who wanted her dead.

They might never find him.

What would happen to her if they didn't?

She couldn't live with Sawyer forever, and she couldn't deny that she had been thinking a lot about the idea of just going home, luring this guy out—assuming he still wanted to kill her—so the cops could arrest him.

Playing bait scared her but no more than living the rest of her life in limbo like this.

She wasn't going to worry about that now though. Now she was going to try to find a little of her Christmas spirit.

"I love this snowman box," she said with a genuinely delighted smile as she picked up a box in the shape of a snowman. It was about fifteen inches tall, with a protruding carrot nose, a big black coal smile, and a black top hat as the lid. It was quite possibly the most adorable thing she had ever seen.

"Told you." Aurora giggled.

"What?" she asked.

"Aurora said that you would pounce on that the second you saw it," Samara explained.

Ashley couldn't help but laugh, her friends knew her so well.

You only had to spend about ten minutes in her presence, and you knew how much she loved snow. Her whole house was—or had been—full of snowmen themed things. From cookie jars to bathrobes, to throw cushions, to art on her walls, her house was her own little personal igloo complete with a whole village full of snowmen to keep her company.

"It's so cute," she gushed, "and it'll be perfect to use for Sawyer's gift." She had spent ages picking out the perfect gift for him this year, something that would go at least a small way toward repaying him for everything he'd done for her. She pulled Sawyer's gift from her own little Santa bag, but then she paused. "Although it would also work well for what I bought for Savannah, too."

Aurora laughed like that was the funniest thing she had ever heard, even serious Samara was smiling.

"What?" she asked, confused.

"I knew you were going to say something like that." Aurora

bounced up and grabbed another bag, pulling out another snowman box, and then another, and another, and another.

She laughed, a real laugh, and it felt so good. "These are just the best thing ever." She beamed. "I think I'm going to keep one for myself." Another round of giggles ensued, and this time she didn't have to ask to know what they were laughing about. "You got me one didn't you?"

Samara reached into her own Santa sack and pulled out one of the snowman boxes. "This is for you, from me and Aurora. I know it's a couple of days early, but we want you to have it now."

Touched, she took the box and opened it up, nestled inside was a gorgeous snowman watch. "Oh, I love it," she said as she pulled it out and immediately put it on. The face of the watch was the snowman's face, the hands were the carrot nose and a pipe, and the watch band had sparkles on it like little snowflakes. She loved sparkly things, she was definitely a glitter kind of girl.

"I'm glad you like it." Samara smiled.

"*Love* it," she corrected. "Thank you so much." She gave both of her friends hugs. "I love you guys so much. I can't thank you enough for being here for me these last few months. I wouldn't have made it without you."

"That's what friends do." Aurora smiled. "Now, let's get wrapping."

Feeling lighter than she had in a long time, Ashley settled down at the table to wrap gifts, chat, and laugh with the people she loved.

∼

10:33 A.M.

He was so frustrated.

Jett hated working a case that he couldn't make progress on, and this one in particular was driving him crazy.

That one of the victims was the woman his wife's twin brother was secretly in love with made things so much worse. He knew how hard this had been on Ashley. Having to give up her life and basically spend twenty-four hours a day, seven days a week, for the last three and a half months sequestered inside Sawyer's house had been beyond rough on her. He wanted to find this guy, he wanted to be able to go to Ashley and tell her that it was over, that she could go back home and back to work, that the threat against her was no longer hanging over her head and she could have her life back.

Instead, he was standing in an alley not far from the one where Ashley had almost lost her life, staring at another dead body.

"You really think this is the same guy?" his partner, Morgan Hawksworth, asked.

Morgan was wrapped up in a thick woolen turtleneck, a coat that made her look like she was about three times her actual size, a scarf wrapped around her neck all the way up to her bottom lip, and a beanie pulled down to just above her eyes. Despite all the layers, Morgan was shivering, his new partner hated the cold, and even though they were yet to get any snow, the weather had been freezing.

He and Morgan had only been partners for the last ten months. His previous partner had gone off the rails and embarked on a killing spree that nearly claimed Savannah's life, and it had been hard to get a new partner. Hard to let himself trust someone else after Blake had taken his trust and decimated it. But he liked Morgan, she was a couple of years younger than him, she was smart, she paid attention to everything anyone said or did, she was good at reading people, and she loved to brainstorm and think outside the box. She was a great partner, and he was glad they were working this case together, maybe she would see something that he and Blake had missed.

"I do," he said, answering Morgan's question.

"He didn't strangle her with a metal chain though," Morgan pointed out.

That was true, but this case was related.

He could feel it.

When he had first started out as an FBI agent, it had taken him a while to learn to trust his instincts. He'd always thought that trusting your gut sounded silly. How could you possibly know whether what you were feeling was to be taken seriously or not? And how could your feelings possibly know anything useful? But he was thirty now, and had been with the FBI for six years and more times than he could count, his gut had saved him or led him to the killer he was hunting.

"He didn't strangle her with a metal chain, but he did strangle her." He crouched beside the body, and careful not to touch anything, pointed at the young woman's neck. "See this, whatever he used he pulled so tight that it left marks actually embedded in her skin, not just a red line. That's just like what he did with the other victims." The killer they were hunting had left scars on Ashley's neck from where the metal chain had dug into her skin when he was strangling her.

"That's true, I guess," Morgan said, sounding unconvinced.

"Same victimology," he added. "Una Attar is twenty-three years old, with long dark hair and dark eyes. That he stuck with the same type of victim tells us something, he needs his victims to look like this which implies that it's for a reason. These women are probably substitutes for someone he knows. He changed what he used to strangle them because he assumes that Ashley told us enough about him that he's scared we're going to find him. But he couldn't change everything. He took the same type of victim, he still strangled them, and he stuck with his same method of grabbing and killing them."

"Okay," Morgan agreed with a nod. "I'm convinced that this is probably the same guy. He's laid low since the attack on Ashley, probably afraid we were going to come for him. But it's been almost four months now, and we haven't, so he obviously felt like it was safe to continue. How long do you think before he takes another victim?"

"Before the break after Ashley, he had been taking less and less time between kills. He killed his first victim over three years ago, he didn't take his second until almost six months later, then another four months before victim number three. It wasn't until victim number four, another four months later, that Blake and I were given the case. He started stepping things up, killing a new woman every couple of months. The last few before Ashley he was barely waiting a couple of weeks between kills. Given that he had to hold off for so long, if we don't find him soon, it might be as little as a couple of days before he goes after someone else. Waiting this long before killing Una had to be hard for him."

"This is the only time he's killed two women in the same city," Morgan said.

Unfortunately, that was true.

So far their killer had kept on the move, one of the reasons it had been so hard to find him. He moved about from city to city, killing only one girl in each before moving on to the next. That he was still here could mean only one thing.

"He's here for Ashley," Jett said simply, it was the only thing that made sense.

"We had it reported that she didn't survive the second attack," Morgan said. "So as far as he knows she's already dead."

"Unless he doesn't believe us," Jett countered. "He could think we're just trying to lull him into a false sense of security, so he doesn't make another attempt on her life. He was interrupted at the hospital when Ashley threw the pad at the glass and knocked it over, sending Sawyer into the room to check on her. The killer had to abandon his attempt to kill her, and he probably knows that he didn't have his hands around her neck long enough to strangle her. Faking Ash's death was always a gamble, and one that's kept her alive for three months, but the only thing that's going to keep her alive is finding this guy."

"It's Christmas time, a time for miracles," Morgan said, rubbing her gloved hands together to warm them.

Last Christmas he had gotten his own miracle, reuniting with the woman he had loved since he'd first laid eyes on her. They had broken up because he hadn't been there for her when she needed him, but he hadn't been able to let her go. He had kept his distance for three years while keeping tabs on her life, and when she had accidentally gotten herself on his ex-partner's radar, and the two of them had been forced to spend time together, they had managed to rekindle what they'd lost.

Now they were happily married.

He was living out his dreams, and he certainly believed that the magic of Christmas had played a big part in his and Savannah's reconciliation.

"There's nothing else we can do here. We just have to hope that ERT finds something useful, or that someone saw something." He didn't hold out much hope that they would get anything from either the crime scene people or a witness. So far this guy had been careful, he hadn't left any forensics behind, and he had come and gone from the murder scenes without anyone seeing him. "We should go to Sawyer's, update him and Ashley on this latest development. If this really is the same guy, then he's back, and just because he's killing other women now doesn't mean he's given up on Ashley. I still believe he intends to come for her, he's just biding his time, and maybe he thinks killing again is a way to speed things up."

"Don't have to tell me twice," Morgan said, already hurrying toward the car. "Anything to get in out of this cold."

Jett rolled his eyes and huffed a chuckle at his partner, then followed her to the car. "You drive," he told her, tossing her the keys. "I want to call and check on Savannah, she wasn't feeling well this morning." While he was hoping that Savannah was feeling better, he really wanted to know if she had taken a pregnancy test. They had been trying to get pregnant since he proposed to her, they both wanted kids, and he was hoping that Savannah feeling sick was, in fact, morning sickness.

Maybe they would all get some good news this Christmas. He and Savannah could get the baby they both wanted so badly, and Ashley could finally get her life back when they took this killer off the streets.

It was the season for miracles after all.

~

10:52 A.M.

The Christmas gifts sitting under the tree looked festive, but even more, Sawyer liked that wrapping gifts and talking with her friends had cheered Ashley up.

She was really due for some good news and Sawyer hoped she got it soon.

He knew that the last three and a half months had been hard for her, having to move out of her home and into his, having to give up work, being cooped up inside all the time, it was a lot for anyone to handle, but so far Ashley had been holding up like a champ. Just like he had known she would. She had days where she struggled, but that was normal, and on the whole she was dealing with everything as best as she could.

Sawyer felt terrible that part of him was enjoying this.

Not the part where a serial rapist and murderer wanted her dead, or the part where she was frustrated about having to put her life on hold, but the part where she was living in his house, and he got to see her every day and spend pretty much all of his time with her, that was exactly what he wanted. He just wished that it was what Ashley wanted as well.

And the bottom line was that none of this was what she wanted.

So many times in the last few months he had considered confessing his feelings for her, but he backed out every time he went to do it. He couldn't see a way to say it without it seeming like he was taking advantage of her, and that was the last thing he wanted to do.

"Santa came a little early this year."

He smiled and turned around to see Ashley standing beside him staring at the tree, a huge grin on her face.

She was such a Christmas girl, she loved it so much, he wished that she could do all the things she usually did.

"Looks like Santa was busy this year," he said, there had to be at least three dozen gifts under the tree. The tree that Ashley hadn't really been particularly keen to decorate. She had asked if they could get some of her decorations from her basement, but he and his bosses had decided it was too risky to make trips back to her house so he'd had to tell her no. She had been disappointed, and he could tell it had taken all the fun of decorating for Christmas away.

"I may have gone a little overboard." Ashley giggled. "Everyone has been so awesome these last few months, and I just wanted to express my appreciation. And at least shopping is something I can still do even if I have to do it here."

He tried not to take the slight curl of her lip and scrunching of her nose when she said the word 'here' personally. Sawyer knew she didn't mean it like that, she just wanted to get her life back, and he couldn't be annoyed with her for that. As much as he loved having her here, and as much as this was way more than just a job for him, he knew that sooner or later it would end. The killer would be caught, Ashley would go back home, and they would go back to being just friends.

Maybe it was time to move on.

He loved Ashley, but she didn't feel the same way, and there was no point in spending the rest of his life pining over someone who didn't want him. He wanted what Savannah had with Jett. He wanted someone who looked at him the way his sister looked at her husband.

"Thanks for insisting we put up the tree, Sawyer." Ashley smiled up at him, her dark eyes sparkling like black diamonds. "I didn't want to, but now I'm so glad we did." She stood on tiptoes and pressed a kiss to his cheek, and he knew it was hopeless. How could he hope to fall in love with someone else when he was already head over heels in love?

Pasting on a smile, he wrapped an arm around Ashley's shoulders, and she immediately leaned into him. "Sometimes, I know you better than you know yourself," he told her.

"You totally do," she agreed and snuggled her head on his shoulder.

She did it so innocently, but she had no idea what that did to him.

It took every bit of willpower he possessed to school his body to calm, and not throw her down in front of the Christmas tree and make love to her.

"I know it's been rough for you lately, but I want you to have a good Christmas," he said.

"I know you do, and so far all things considered, it's pretty awesome. We have a beautiful tree, and the presents underneath make it look even better. Now all we need is for it to snow."

The Santa Clause movies immediately popped into his head. They had been his and Savannah's favorites when they were kids, and they had watched them together with their parents every single Christmas Eve. The scene where Scott Calvin was picking up Carol Newman for their date, and he was driving her in the horse-drawn sleigh, and he made it snow for her, had been Savannah's favorite, and Sawyer wished he had his own magical watch that he could use to create snow for Ashley.

While that was impossible, he did have the next best thing.

"I have something for you, I'd been holding off, hoping I wouldn't need it and I'd be able to give it to you as a joke on Christmas morning, but since we're having a nice Christmassy day, I'm going to give it to you now."

"What is it?" Ashley demanded, practically glowing with enthusiasm. It was like the old Ashley was back today, he hoped she stayed, he'd missed her.

"You'll find out in just a moment."

Leaving Ashley in the living room, he went out to the garage and grabbed the bag he'd hidden out there a couple of weeks ago.

"What is that?" Ashley's brow scrunched in confusion when he came back.

"Snow," he replied.

"Snow?"

"Fake snow. Since you've been complaining that we haven't had any snow yet and that it doesn't feel like Christmas without it, I bought you this."

"Oh, Sawyer, that is the sweetest thing ever," she gushed, rushing over to throw her arms around his neck and plant another kiss on his cheek. "How does it work?"

"Well, according to the instructions, we just add water, and it expands to make snow."

"Let's make it now. What should we put it in?"

"What about we mix it up in the bathtub."

"Okay." Ashley ran ahead of him up the stairs, and he couldn't help but smile. When she was happy he was happy, when she was suffering he was suffering, and now that her mood had lifted so had his.

"You know it doesn't stick together like real snow," he warned, not wanting to dampen her spirits, but he didn't want her to think this was going to be exactly the same as real snow. "We won't be able to make snowmen or snowballs or anything."

"I don't care, this is so cool," she said as they both knelt beside the bath.

Sawyer couldn't help but laugh, she was acting like a little kid, and he loved it. This was as excited as she got over real snow. They figured out how much water they needed for the amount of fake snow powder they had and added it to the bathtub, almost immediately it began to expand. It really did look just like snow, and when you touched it, it even felt almost like snow, the soft, light, fluffy kind.

"Ooh, it's so awesome," Ashley said, sticking her hands straight in it and letting it flutter through her fingertips. "This is the best gift ever. I'm so glad you didn't wait until Christmas Day to give it to me."

"I'm glad you like it so much."

"*Love* it," she corrected.

While Ashley ran her hands through it, and piled it up in little towers and knocked them down again, he just sat back and watched her. He couldn't help but feel good that he'd made her smile like that. He knew it wasn't ever going to be anything other than friendship between them, but moments like this when Ashley was smiling and happy made knowing he would never be with her the way he wanted more than worth it. He was lucky to have her as a friend, and part of him didn't want to do anything that could ruin that.

What if he asked her out and she said yes and they dated, but it didn't work out. Then he wouldn't just be losing his girlfriend but his best friend as well because things would never be able to go back to this if they dated and then broke up.

"Sawyer."

He looked up and got a face full of fake snow.

~

11:24 A.M.

Ashley laughed as her fake snow snowball exploded in Sawyer's face.

Like he'd said, the fake snow didn't really stick together, but she didn't care, it was still fun to play with.

Quickly she picked up another handful and tossed it at Sawyer.

"Oh, you just started a war, missy," he said as he reached into the bath and picked up his own handful of snow.

She squealed and tried to dodge away and hide behind the vanity, but Sawyer was too quick, and a handful of snow got her in the side of the face. "You want a war you got one." She giggled as she ducked back to the bath to grab more snow.

Just as she picked up a handful, Sawyer got her with another snowball of his own. "I think I'm winning, that's my three to your two." He laughed.

"Oh yeah?" She reached into the bath and gathered up an entire armful and threw it at Sawyer.

"You'll pay for that one," he said as he brushed the snow off his face. Sawyer came at her, and as she tried to grab more snow he picked her up and dangled her over the bath. "In you go."

"Don't you dare," she squawked as she wrapped her arms around his neck.

"Oh, I dare," he goaded.

"You wouldn't," she said, trying to squirm out of his grip. She knew her friend, and she knew he was going to do it.

"In you go," Sawyer said, lowering her down so he didn't hurt her, then dropping her at the last moment into the huge pile of soft, fluffy snow.

He thought he had won.

But he was wrong.

Ashley didn't release the death grip she had on Sawyer's shoulders, and her weight overbalanced him, and he toppled down along with her, landing awkwardly on top of her.

"Sorry, Ash," he said, immediately trying to lever his weight back off her.

"I'm not." She laughed and held on to him. All the depression that had been weighing her down earlier this morning had evaporated. Hanging out with her friends and wrapping gifts, then playing with Sawyer and his fabulous gift was just what she needed. Sure she still wished that Jett and Morgan would hurry up and find the killer, but she was getting to spend time with her best friend who had done so much, and continued to do so much for her.

She was one lucky girl, and she should act like it.

Not everyone had people in their life who would sacrifice their time just to help them when they needed it.

And sixteen other young women hadn't been as lucky as her.

Sixteen other young women had died at the hands of the same killer she had managed to survive twice.

However long it took for the FBI to find him at least she was safe, she had to keep focusing on that and not on what she had lost.

Pressing a kiss to Sawyer's cheek, she hugged him hard. "You are the very best friend that anyone could ever ask for."

"Right back at ya." He smiled down at her.

Her gaze dropped from his eyes to his lips, and she sucked in a surprised breath when she realized she wanted to kiss him.

Whoa.

Where had that come from?

She and Sawyer had been friends for years, they spent a lot of time together, and never once had she ever wanted to kiss him.

Until now.

It was probably just because they had spent excessive amounts of time together since he'd become her bodyguard. He had been so sweet with her, so thoughtful, so kind, he had given her exactly what she needed and usually knew what she needed even before she did. And then today was like the icing on the cake. He knew how much she loved snow and how sad she was that there hadn't been any so far this year, and the fake snow was just the most amazing thing ever. She was going to get this stuff every Christmas regardless of whether or not there was real snow.

That was probably why she wanted to kiss him.

Nothing more.

Slowly her eyes moved from Sawyer's lips to his eyes and saw they were heated and locked onto hers.

This was wrong.

She couldn't kiss her best friend.

That would ruin everything.

Ashley knew that, and yet almost of their own accord, her lips parted and she drew in a shaky half nervous half lustful breath. Like they were two glowing blue magnets, Sawyer's eyes held on to hers, and his head dipped slightly.

It looked like bad idea or not, this was going to happen.

She lifted her head to meet his and the doorbell rang.

Sawyer immediately straightened. "I better go see who that is."

"Yeah," she agreed, disappointed. She had *wanted* to kiss Sawyer, but this was probably for the best. If they kissed there was no turning back, it would irrevocably change things, and right now, Sawyer was the only stable thing she had in her life, and she didn't know what she would do without him. Still, despite all of that, she couldn't deny that it would have been amazing. Sawyer was hot with his messy dark blond hair and bright blue eyes, broad shoulders, muscular arms, and those abs of his were the most drool-worthy she'd ever seen.

This was for the best.

For.

The.

Best.

"Yeah, keep telling yourself that," she muttered to herself as she trailed down the stairs after Sawyer.

As she reached the living room, Sawyer was just locking the door behind Jett and Morgan.

Like a bucket of ice water had been dumped on her head, her good mood evaporated.

She knew why the FBI agents were here, it was written all over their faces.

They had bad news.

Since they weren't smiling and all excited, they weren't here to tell her that the man who had tried to kill her twice already was either dead or in custody. So that left only one other reason they'd be here in the middle of the day. The killer had claimed another victim.

"What's with you two and this weird white stuff?" Jett asked as they all took seats in the living room.

Ashley looked down at herself and saw that there were flakes of the fake snow all over her clothes, and she had no doubt they were all over her face and in her hair as well. "We had a snowball fight," she said with a small smile, and glanced over at Sawyer to find him watching her closely.

Was he thinking about their almost kiss?

Should they talk about it?

There wasn't really anything to talk about, but if the doorbell hadn't rung when it did, there would definitely have been.

And Ashley wasn't sure it would have stopped with just a kiss.

She was pretty sure it would have ended with the two of them in bed together.

She wasn't even sure she would have regretted it.

But she did still think it would have been a mistake. Sleeping with Sawyer could mean losing him, and besides, she didn't even know that it was what he wanted. It looked like he wanted to kiss her too, but maybe she was just seeing what she wanted to see.

"We were playing with some fake snow," Sawyer told the FBI Agents. "So, what's going on?"

"We wanted to let you know in person that we think the killer took another victim last night." Jett broke the news as gently as he could, telling her exactly what she had been expecting to hear.

Her heart dropped.

This was another reminder of exactly how grateful she should be and how lucky she had been.

She had come so close—twice—to ending up like this poor woman.

"Do you have anything helpful from the scene?" she asked. Surely they must have something by now. How could this guy have killed seventeen women, plus almost kill her twice, and yet they had nothing on him?

"Sorry, Ash, so far we don't have anything, but ERT is still going over the scene, if he left anything behind, we'll find it," Jett told her.

It wasn't that she thought the FBI wasn't doing their job, she knew they were. She knew that Jett and Morgan were working this case every second they could, even when their caseload was high they kept the case a priority, but she was starting to feel like this was never going to end.

Was this going to be her life now?

Stuck indoors pretty much around the clock, with someone babysitting her, unable to work or even just go out and have fun?

This was too much right now.

"Thanks for coming all the way over here to tell me," she said to Jett and Morgan. "I think I'm going to go upstairs and clean up."

~

11:49 A.M.

"You guys have the worst timing," Sawyer muttered at Jett and Morgan as Ashley disappeared up the stairs.

"Sorry," Morgan said.

"You guys were having fun with your snow thing, huh?" Jett asked.

"You have no idea." Not only had Ashley been more relaxed than he'd seen her since this nightmare started having fun and laughing, but she'd been going to kiss him.

Sawyer still couldn't believe it, but he'd seen it in her eyes.

She'd been staring at his lips, and when she'd lifted her gaze to meet his eyes, her lips had parted, and she had lifted her head to meet his.

But then the doorbell had rung, breaking the moment.

He wasn't sure whether he should hope for another moment or not. Ashley had wanted to kiss him because she had gotten caught up in the moment. From wrapping gifts to playing with the fake snow, she'd been having fun and feeling Christmassy, and the almost kiss had just grown out of that. But for him it was different. For him it went so much deeper. He had real feelings for Ashley and taking that leap of faith was scary because he knew she didn't feel the same way about him.

"So," he said, focusing on his job for the moment. As much as he'd love to get back to Ashley and try to cheer her up again, right now keeping her alive had to be the priority. Yes, he loved having her stay with him because he liked her, but he couldn't allow himself to forget why she was here. One slip up on his part, and he could lose Ashley forever. "You think this is a statement on the killer's part? You think he's back and he wants us to know it?"

"He didn't follow his MO to the letter," Morgan said. "Victim fits with his others, as does the way he grabbed her, while he did strangle her, this time he didn't use a chain. Jett is convinced it's the same guy, so we think maybe he tried to use a different tool to kill her so that we might not link it to him."

"So you think he wants to keep killing and not get caught so he's mixing things up? You don't think that this is an attempt to throw us off our game and let our guards down so that he can make a play for Ashley?" Sawyer asked.

"I don't think he's given up on Ashley," Jett said. "He stayed here. This is the first time he's ever tried to take two victims in the same city. Since he made the choice to stay here, I think that means there's something holding him here. That something has to be Ashley. I think that he wants us to think since he laid low for nearly four months that was him wanting to get to Ashley, and now that he's started killing again that means he's moved on."

"Then this isn't over." As much as he loved having her here and was going to miss her when she moved back to her own house, he wanted this over. He didn't like living, knowing someone wanted the woman he loved dead. This man had already done enough to Ashley, he'd taken her self-confidence, he'd taken her sense of safety and security, he'd taken away a part of her when he raped her that she could never get back, he wasn't going to take her life.

"No, it's not," Morgan said, her green eyes full of sympathy.

"I know we keep saying this and yet not backing it up with results, but we're doing everything we can to get this guy so Ashley can get her life back," Jett added.

"I know you are," he assured the two agents. He knew they were sacrificing time with family to work this case, and he appreciated it more than he could express. "I better get up there and check on Ashley. Thanks for the update, and thanks for delivering it in person."

"You're welcome." Morgan smiled. "Ashley is really lucky to have you. And I don't just mean as her bodyguard, but as her friend too."

Did he just get a vibe from her?

Was she interested in him?

Morgan was stunning with wavy red hair and gorgeous green eyes, she was sweet and dedicated to her job, they would probably make a good couple, but he was already in love with someone else so it wasn't fair to pursue anything with her knowing that.

Hopefully, he had just read her wrong, he didn't want to have to turn her down, he would, it was just never a fun thing to have to do.

"Thanks." He smiled back, trying to make the smile neutral, he didn't want to lead her on.

"As always, we'll keep you updated," Jett said.

Sawyer showed the agents out, closing the door behind them and locking it. He reset the security alarm, then headed upstairs to find Ashley. He found her in the bathroom cleaning up the mess they had made earlier. "You doing okay?"

Ashley just shrugged.

"Jett and Morgan will find this guy," he reminded her. He knew the words sounded empty after nearly four months and no progress on the case, but he didn't know what else to say.

"Sure," came the mumbled reply, and she wouldn't look up from the broom she was using to sweep up the fake snow that was sprinkled all over the bathroom.

"Really, Ash, sooner or later they'll get him, hopefully sooner rather than later but it will happen."

Finally she stopped what she was doing.

She didn't turn around, and he didn't push her, she needed time to process this new information.

After a solid minute or more she slowly turned. The sparkle that had been there just thirty minutes ago was gone from her eyes, and the smile was gone from her face. Instead she looked scared, sad, and frustrated. "Can you promise me that one day this will end?"

He knew she knew the answer to that, but he said it anyway. "No, I can't. I wish I could, but no one can guarantee the future."

"So this could never be over. This could be my life."

"It could," he agreed.

"I'm so sick of this," she said helplessly.

"I know you are, honey."

"I want it to end. I want him caught. Really I want him dead. Does that make me a bad person?" she asked anxiously.

"Of course not. This man has raped and murdered seventeen young women. He tried to kill you twice." He purposely didn't remind her that he had raped her too, it was still a very sensitive subject for her, which he completely understood. He didn't feel equipped to help her deal with that, if she wanted to talk about it he would listen, but he didn't want to initiate a conversation about it if it wasn't what she wanted.

"Thanks for being honest with me," Ashley said.

"Always. What can I do to help cheer you up?" Whatever it took he would gladly do.

"You do cheer me up." She smiled. "You always cheer me up. I don't know how I'm ever going to repay you for everything you've done for me."

"Why would you need to repay me? We're best friends, I'm only doing what anyone would do in this situation."

"Well, I love you for it." She came over and wrapped her arms around his waist, resting her cheek on his chest. Her hair tickled his nose, and he couldn't help but breathe in her scent, she smelled like the lavender-scented shampoo she always used.

Holding her like this was such a dichotomy. It was everything he ever wanted, and yet it was also torture. It was like having the carrot dangled in front of him but not being able to reach it.

Pulling up his big boy shorts, he wrapped his arms around her and gave her the comfort she needed, just like he had done every other time she had needed it over the last few months, and would do every other time she needed it.

"Love you too, babe," he said. "Why don't you go grab a shower in your bathroom, and I'll finish cleaning up in here then we can have lunch."

She held on to him a moment longer then straightened her spine. That was his girl, it didn't matter how many times life tried to shove her down she always came back stronger than ever. "Yeah, okay. Thanks again, Sawyer."

"Stop with all the thank yous. Now go." He swatted her bottom and gently pushed her in the direction of the door.

"I'm going." She gave a small laugh as she headed out the door.

Sawyer watched her go, it was possible he loved her even more every time he saw her strength. He was both the luckiest and the unluckiest guy in the world to be living with the woman he loved and yet not have her as his own.

~

9:54 P.M.

The nights were the worst.

It was easier in the daytime to keep her spirits up, stay busy, and let the people around her keep her distracted.

But at night, alone in bed, Ashley couldn't help but dwell.

Tonight she was feeling particularly depressed, which was a shame after the great morning she'd had.

Jett and Morgan's visit had changed everything.

Maybe it was naïve of her, but she had really started to believe that the killer had bought their charade of faking her death, and so with her no longer a threat to him had simply moved on. It wasn't that she wanted more women to die, she wanted this guy caught or dead. With him still out there she would probably never sleep through the night again—even if he was captured or killed she might not—but she also wanted her life back.

Now that dream was over.

The killer hadn't moved on like she had hoped, he was still here, so he probably knew he hadn't been in her hospital room long enough to kill her, which meant he still wanted to finish what he had started, therefore she was stuck here indefinitely.

That wasn't the news she wanted to hear.

She wanted to be back in her adorable little cottage with the cute dormer windows and the bright yellow siding with white trim. She wanted to be in her own bedroom, painted a soothing pale blue, with the fancy chandelier that hung over her bed. She wanted to be back in her own bed, with her soft mattress, and her fluffy feather pillows, and her favorite patchwork quilt, the one she and her mom had made one particularly cold, snowy winter when she was a child.

Tears seeped from her eyes, and she quickly wiped them away.

She didn't want to be ungrateful, but she couldn't expect Sawyer to have her stay here forever. Sooner or later he would get tired of this around the clock babysitting and want to get back to his own life. What if he fell for someone and things got serious, and they wanted to move in together? She couldn't expect the other woman to want to have her around.

Then what would happen to her?

There were other bodyguards who worked with the company, she would probably have to go and stay with one of them. But what happened when they wanted to move on with their lives? Would she just keep getting shuffled from place to place, moving on when people got tired of her? What kind of life was that?

Maybe it would be easier for everyone if she just moved someplace else and started over with a new name and a new identity.

She didn't really want to because she would be leaving behind everything she loved, but in a way she already had. She had given up everything already so it shouldn't be that hard to say goodbye and move on.

Except leaving would mean leaving Sawyer.

And she wasn't sure she could do that.

Which was selfish of her. She was keeping both their lives in limbo by staying here.

What if this was all for nothing?

What if the killer had already decided it wasn't worth the risk of getting caught just for another chance at ending her life?

As much as Ashley wanted to believe that, she didn't. The look in his eyes in that hospital room when he wrapped his hands around her throat was one of sheer determination.

Absently, her hands lifted to touch her neck, tracing the indents in the skin that would forever be a reminder of what she had been through.

She hated those scars.

Those first few days after the attack her throat had burned every time she swallowed, pretty much every time she breathed. Eating had been too hard, and she had lost several pounds in the couple of weeks where all she could eat was cold soups and protein shakes. It had been five days before she'd been able to speak and even then it had hurt.

Her throat had suffered a lot of damage, but it had healed.

The marks from the metal chain hadn't.

Even now, coming up on four months since the assault and they were still bright red, drawing your attention straight to them like a beacon.

Ashley didn't like for anyone to see them so she kept them covered under a scarf at all times, only taking it off when she climbed into bed each night. Even Sawyer who was with her twenty-four hours a day hadn't seen them since she left the hospital. She didn't know if she would ever get to a place where she was comfortable enough with anyone to let them see her scars.

Her fingers were still convulsively tracing the indentations when she heard a noise.

She bolted upright and reached over to switch on the lamp on the nightstand beside the bed.

Was someone there?

No one should be able to get in here, Sawyer's house had a top of the line security system, and Sawyer himself was here.

She knew from experience that any little sound would wake him up. There were plenty of nights where unable to sleep, she had gotten up to go downstairs to the kitchen to make herself a snack, or to watch some TV, or read, or anything really that meant she didn't have to go to sleep. Any time she did that, no matter how quiet she thought she was, Sawyer always woke up and came to join her.

If someone was in here, Sawyer would know.

Her ears strained, trying to hear something through the near crushing silence.

She had grown to hate silence.

Silence was when bad thoughts crept into your head. When memories that most of the time you were able to keep locked away suddenly seemed to find the key and sneak back out. Silence was when you felt so alone that you almost couldn't bear it. Silence was fear.

She should have asked Sawyer to sleep in here with her tonight. She should have known that Jett and Morgan's news was going to dredge up all her memories of the attack that had almost ended her life, but instead just irrevocably changed it. After being discharged from the hospital, Sawyer had slept in a sleeping bag on the floor beside her bed when she had first moved in here. She had been too afraid to be alone and had even made him sit outside the bathroom door, with the door open, while she took a shower, trusting that he wouldn't look at her.

She could go now, knock on his door, ask him to come and sleep in here tonight because she was afraid.

But she didn't.

Because of what had happened earlier.

Wanting to kiss Sawyer changed everything. It moved him out of the friend zone and put him in the potential boyfriend zone. And she really didn't want to do that. She needed him too much to do anything that would risk losing him.

Now she couldn't feel comfortable with Sawyer sleeping in her room, even on the floor.

The kiss that never even happened had already changed things.

Another noise made her jump.

Her heart raced and her pulse hammered in her ears. It took her a good minute to realize that it was just a car driving down the street.

Comfortable or not she couldn't spend the night alone.

Throwing the covers back, she grabbed her pillow and the quilt and climbed out of bed, half expecting the monster who had lived under her bed when she was a child to reach out his claws and grab her. She padded across the thick carpet to the door and then tiptoed across the hall to Sawyer's room.

Easing the door open as carefully as she could so she didn't make a sound, she snuck inside. She didn't want to wake Sawyer, she just didn't want to be alone, and maybe sleeping on the floor in his room instead of him sleeping on the floor in her room made things less complicated.

Or not.

She didn't know, she was way too tired, and she couldn't think straight right now.

As she stretched out on the floor at the end of Sawyer's bed, resting her head on her pillow and wrapping the quilt around her, Ashley knew only one thing.

Sawyer made her feel safe.

It was as simple as that.

She didn't know if that meant it was worth risking their friendship to find out if there could be something more between them, or whether or not she would stay here until the killer was found however long that might be, or whether moving and starting over somewhere else was the best option. She just knew what she felt.

Exhausted, Ashley closed her eyes and drifted off to sleep, safe in the knowledge that Sawyer was here.

~

10:38 P.M.

It was time to move on.

He couldn't live in limbo forever.

He wanted Ashley Fallon dead, but he also had to satisfy the beast inside him. The beast was relentless, it craved things it shouldn't, and he wasn't strong enough to stand up to it.

He was a coward.

He always had been, and he always would be.

He had grown to accept that. He was who he was, he couldn't change it, and even if he could he wasn't sure that he would. He and the beast had some things in common, and every time he took another life they were both satiated.

At least for a time.

But it never lasted.

Whenever he thought that he had his cravings under control he found that he didn't. And that was what you were supposed to do, right? You were supposed to embrace who you were and not be ashamed of it. Self-worth, self-esteem, self-confidence, that was what his therapist always used to be harping on about.

So that was what he had done.

He had found a way to repair the damage done to him, and now he did have self-worth, self-esteem, and self-confidence.

There was one person who held the power to destroy all of that.

Ashley Fallon.

He hadn't known her name at first or cared about it, it wasn't important to him that he knew the identities of the women who fed his needs. But this one was different. This one had survived.

He still wasn't really sure how that had happened.

In his mind he kept replaying that night over and over again, trying to pinpoint what mistake he had made.

Maybe it was that she had been on the phone.

It wasn't the first time he had taken a woman who had been on the phone at the time. It was pretty hard not to because most people were on their phones most of the time. He hated that. He thought phones were one of the reasons why the world had fallen apart like it had. Other times he'd grabbed a woman on a phone it had gone fine. Sure, he knew that the person on the other end would know something had happened, but that didn't affect things.

Only that time with Ashley it had.

Somehow, whoever she had been on the phone with had known exactly where she was. There must have been a cop car close by because he'd heard sirens before he was done.

It had been a struggle to leave.

He so badly wanted to stay and make sure she was dead, but he couldn't risk getting caught, so he had climbed a fence to get out of the alley and had thankfully been gone before the cops arrived.

Since they didn't know who he was, he had hung around and followed the ambulance to the hospital. He knew he had to take her out. She had seen him. He never bothered to wear a mask or anything when he made his kills, there wasn't really any point, they were never going to be able to tell anyone what they had seen.

But this one could.

Once he got to the hospital, it had taken him a while to find the woman he was looking for. He had to steal some scrubs so he looked the part of the doctor, and it seemed to work because no one bothered to give him a second glance.

All his hard work had paid off and he'd found Ashley's name, then what room she was in, and then he'd been able to walk right in.

It should have been so easy.

He had her.

He *had* her.

She was completely at his mercy, in a hospital bed, hooked up to IVs, with a tube looped across her face helping deliver additional oxygen to her, and yet still she had managed to best him. She'd had something in her hands, and she must have used it to throw at the glass and knock it down, making sure someone came running to her aid once again.

And once again he had to flee before the job was done.

At least he'd managed to make it out of the hospital.

He had moved quickly, and luck had for once been on his side. The man who'd come running in to save Ashley—he assumed the same man who had been on the phone with her earlier—had wanted to make sure that she was alive and that had given him the head start he needed. He'd ditched the scrubs and slipped away unnoticed.

They thought they were so smart.

They'd tried to trick him, make him think that his second attempt at killing Ashley was successful, but he wasn't an idiot. He knew that he hadn't been in there long enough to kill her. It took a good several minutes to strangle someone to death, a fact he hadn't been aware of the first time he'd done it. That had very nearly become a disaster. The woman had passed out, he'd thought he'd done it and it was over and had already started to clean up, then he'd looked up and seen the woman dragging herself toward the street.

After that he was careful.

Very careful.

He checked and rechecked to make sure that the women were dead before he left. And Ashley Fallon hadn't been dead when he left that hospital room.

Their ruse hadn't worked.

He knew Ashley was still alive, they had just hidden her away someplace where he wouldn't be able to find her. And he hadn't.

For the first month he had kept up a vigil outside her home, having managed to find her address, but she never showed up. Then he had tried to learn as much about her as he could, but it was hard. He couldn't just openly go about asking questions about her. So he had started at the restaurant she had been at that night, he knew which one it was because he had seen the takeout bag in her hand. That hadn't yielded much but more than he'd had before. He learned she loved to work out and adored Christmas time, usually buying a lot of decorations from a small store just down the block. He had staked out the restaurant and the Christmas store but had yet to see her at either. Since she couldn't attend the gym he had been jogging in the parks a couple of times a day, hoping to catch a glimpse of her.

So far he hadn't.

Whoever was keeping her locked away was doing a good job.

They were persistent.

But he was more persistent.

She was his only failure, and he needed to rectify that.

Yet, at the same time, it was time to move on. He couldn't just spend all his time trying to find Ashley Fallon. Sooner or later they would slip up or become complacent, and then he would pounce.

Until then the beast needed to be fed.

Last night he had gone out hunting. It felt good to be out and about again instead of just sitting and waiting. He would get Ashley, but he was going to move on and keep living his life as well.

He wondered if the cops thought he had given up on her.

He hoped they did. He hoped they thought he was no longer a threat to Ashley and send her back home so he could swoop in and get her. He had tried to throw them off his trail, confuse them, by giving up the metal chain and using a rope instead. The chain held a certain sentimental appeal but not to the point that he would keep using it if there was something better he could do. He didn't really care if they thought last night's kill was or wasn't him, all he cared about was throwing them into confusion.

Confused people did stupid things.

He should know.

He had been confused once upon a time, and he had lived to regret it.

He had spent the rest of his life making amends in the only way he knew how.

While once he had seen as if through a heavy fog, he now saw clearly. He knew what he was doing, and he knew what he wanted, and nothing was going to stop him from getting it. Certainly not a bunch of cops.

Leaving his house he stepped out into the night.

The beast liked the night, it liked the dark, it hated the light, the sun, the noise, and clutter. So he slept during the day and roamed at night in the freedom the dark afforded.

Closing the door behind him, he strolled out in the moonlight, content in the knowledge that one day Ashley Fallon's life would be squeezed out of her by his hands, and until that day came, there would be many others who would give their lives to him and his beast.

CHAPTER

Four

December 22nd
5:15 A.M.

His bedroom door opened quietly.

The sound snapped him from sleep, and Sawyer kept himself still but cracked an eye open.

Ashley, with her pillow and quilt in her arms, was slipping out of his room.

He was always a light sleeper, but even more so when he was working so he knew she had crept in here around ten-thirty last night, but since she hadn't woken him up she obviously hadn't wanted him to know that she was there, so he hadn't said anything. He had assumed that she was scared and having trouble sleeping after learning that the man who had tried to kill her twice had struck again and just hadn't wanted to be alone.

Sawyer wished she had woken him up and told him that, he would have gotten up and had a late-night snack with her, talked, watched movies, or played card games or whatever she wanted to do to take her mind off things. At the very least he would have slept on the floor in her room so that she could have slept in a bed. Before, when she had needed company she had always told him, he wondered what had changed.

He could make a guess.

He'd almost kissed her, and obviously that had shifted something between them.

Hopefully, it hadn't ruined their friendship.

He couldn't let that happen again. Even after this case was closed and he was no longer her bodyguard he couldn't try to kiss her.

Friends.

They were friends.

Nothing more and nothing less.

And it was definitely better than nothing.

Sawyer climbed out of bed, he hadn't done more than doze since Ashley tiptoed into his room and lay down at the end of his bed, and he certainly wouldn't sleep knowing she was up, so he may as well get up too. He could hear Ashley moving about in her room. She sounded restless. She was sick of being cooped up inside, and she wasn't the only one. As much as he loved spending all his time with her, he would much rather be spending that time out and about, not stuck inside twenty-four hours a day.

A glance at the clock on his nightstand told him it was quarter past five, it should be safe enough to take her out for a quick jog around the park near his house.

Throwing on sweats, he went and knocked on her door.

"Sorry, did I wake you?" she asked when she opened it.

"You know I'm an early riser," he said to put her at ease, he didn't want her worrying about how much sleep he was getting. He had never been one to need a lot of sleep, something which definitely came in handy with his job. "Since we're both up, and I know you've been going stir crazy stuck inside, how about we go for a jog?"

Her dark eyes lit up. "Really?"

"Would I kid with you about that?"

"No," she said, shaking her head and sending her long dark hair splashing over her shoulders. What he wouldn't give to run his fingers through that hair, then wrap it around his hand and bring her face to his and kiss her senseless.

No.

Stop, he chided himself.

Friends.

They were friends.

"So, you want to go?"

"Of course." She clapped her hands delightedly. "Give me five minutes to get dressed, and I'll meet you downstairs."

While he waited, Sawyer headed downstairs, put his sneakers on, and grabbed his gun from the safe. Sure an early morning run should be safe enough, and the killer obviously didn't know that Ashley was staying here because no attempts on her life had been made, but he couldn't be too careful, not when he was dealing with the life of the woman he loved.

"I'm ready," Ashley announced, just as he was grabbing water bottles from the fridge.

He turned around to find her grinning at him, dressed in a pair of pink sweats that hung off her curvy hips and a purple sweater that clung to her breasts and left nothing to the imagination. He very nearly had to open the bottles and dump the cold water on himself, but he was a grown man, and he could control himself. Barely, but he could, especially since he knew sex with him wasn't what Ashley wanted and would only end up pushing her away.

"Great," he said brightly, handing her one of the bottles of water. "Let's go."

"Where are we going to run?" she asked as they headed out into the crisp morning. Despite the fact that it was now officially winter, and Christmas was just a couple of days away, the sky was clear, and it looked like they were in for another cold but sunny day with no chance of snow.

"I thought we'd run the circuit in the park just a few streets over. It's nice and quiet, and the scenery is great. There're a few hills and lots of trees, it'll make a nice change from the house."

"It sure will," she agreed.

Sawyer started off in the direction of the park, keeping his pace slow and steady, they both ran on his treadmill every day, but there was a difference between running indoors on the treadmill and running outdoors on the sidewalk. Ashley kept pace beside him, and he could practically feel the excitement vibrating off her.

It didn't take much to make her happy.

Even before the assault she hadn't been one of those girls who fussed over things, who wanted to be the center of attention, bragged about things, and acted like a drama queen when they didn't get their way. Ashley was calm and easy-going, which was why they always had so much fun together.

As a kid, he had lost sight of fun for a while.

His dad had died when he was ten, in a car accident while he'd been driving Savannah someplace. The car had gone off the road, and had trapped their father inside. Injured but determined, Savannah had walked a mile to the nearest house to get help. Unfortunately, by the time she returned with help it was already too late.

That event had shaped the person his twin sister had become, filling her with a need to save others as though she had to make up for failing to save their father. It was a trait that had nearly gotten her killed on several occasions.

Although he hadn't been there, that event had shaped his life as well. It was the reason he had trained to become a bodyguard, he liked protecting people, it made him feel like he was making a difference in the world. It had also turned him from an easy-going kid to one who was much more serious as he took on the role of man of the house, looking out for his mother and sister.

But when he was with Ashley he felt like he could relax, let his guard down a little. That protectiveness was still there, fiercer than ever where Ash was concerned, but her calm, fun-loving nature rubbed off on him.

"There's the park," Ashley announced, picking up her speed a little as they rounded the corner and the park came into view.

Sawyer matched her pace, and a minute later they were entering the park. This park in particular was one of his favorites of the four that were near his house. It wasn't so much a kid's park, there were no playgrounds or soccer fields or anything like that. It was mostly just woodland spread over a square mile, with a small lake, thousands of trees, and several running tracks. Whenever he came here it was like he'd left the city behind and entered a whole other world.

From the small content smile that lit Ashley's face, it was clear she felt the same way. Maybe he'd try to take her jogging here every morning.

"You want to take the trail that goes around the outside of the park or the one that weaves through? Or we could go the lake route," he added, thinking the smooth water could be nice to run around.

"Which is the longest?"

"The one that weaves through."

"Let's do that one then."

"The longest route it is," he said, knowing that Ashley wanted to make the most of this time out of the house.

He took off down the middle path, Ashley at his side. Although it was only five-thirty in the morning and freezing cold out, a few other people were walking or running. A few had dogs, one woman had a stroller with her, he surveyed each person carefully, but none appeared to pose any threat to Ashley.

They weaved along through the trees. He slowed his pace as they headed up a hill in case it was too much for Ashley, but she showed no signs of slowing, it was like the fun of being outside had given her extra energy.

Just as they were about to reach the top of the hill, Ashley suddenly darted off ahead, "Bet I beat you to the end of the track," she squealed over her shoulder.

"Hey, Ash, don't get too far ahead," he cautioned, picking up his pace to catch up to her, he didn't think she was unsafe here, but he didn't want to take any chances.

"Don't be such a—" Ashley broke off with a scream.

Panic spurred him on, and he reached the top of the hill in seconds, but there was no sign of Ashley anywhere.

∽

5:36 A.M.

.   .   .

As her feet flew out from underneath her, Ashley screamed.

She had rolled her ankle on something and lost her balance, and now she was careening down the side of the hill.

There were trees everywhere, and she was terrified that she was going to smash her head into one and kill herself or snap her neck.

Rocks and sticks were catching her on the way down, tearing at her skin and leaving bruises she knew would take weeks to heal.

If she didn't kill herself first.

How clumsy could she be?

It seemed like she was rolling in slow motion, the decline was only around twenty feet and pretty steep, surely she should have hit the ground by now.

"Ashley?" Sawyer called out her name.

That distracted her enough that she moved her arms, which she had been using to cover her face as best she could, and her head slammed into a tree.

She saw stars.

Literally.

Bright, shiny stars.

She landed with a thud at the bottom, the air whooshed from her lungs.

"Ashley? Where are you?"

Sawyer.

She needed to tell him what had happened.

He probably thought the killer had snatched her, but nope, it was just her being her usual clumsy self.

Because she didn't want to worry her best friend she somehow staggered to her feet. "Down here," she called out, her voice sounding as spaced out as she felt.

"Ash? You're down where? Down the hill? Did you fall?"

"I tripped, rolled my ankle."

"Are you okay? Are you hurt?"

She thought she could see him at the top of the hill, but she wasn't sure, her vision was a little blurry, and it was still mostly dark out. "I'm a little banged up but okay," she called up.

"I'm coming down."

"Don't come down the hill, there are too many trees, you'll get hurt." That was the last thing they needed for both of them to get hurt.

"I'll circle around on the path then come down and find you. Don't move okay? Stay put, it might take me a couple of minutes, but I'm coming."

"Yeah, okay," she agreed.

"I mean it, don't move."

Ashley could hear the fear in his voice, and she knew it was half because he was worried that she was more seriously hurt than she had said, and half because it terrified him to have her out of his sight. She knew he was every bit as afraid of the killer coming after her again as she was. And she was every bit as anxious for him to get to her as he was to get to her.

She sagged against the nearest tree, unable to remain upright.

She felt drained.

Her bad ankle wobbled, and she used the tree for support as she sunk to the ground and laid her head back against the trunk, stretching her injured leg out in front of her.

She was starting to shake, a mixture of the cold and anxiety. She couldn't believe it, but she wanted to go back to Sawyer's. After months of complaining—even if it was inwardly just to herself—about being cooped up and unable to go out, she actually wished she had stayed at home today. She wished they had never come out for a jog. When Sawyer had suggested it she had pounced on it, thrilled for any chance to be paroled, even temporarily.

Now she would give anything to be back home.

Home.

It was funny, but she was starting to think of Sawyer's house as her home.

As much as she still wanted to go back to her house, she couldn't deny that Sawyer's house now felt like home. It felt safe, and she was comfortable there, if she couldn't live at her own house then the only other place she would want to be was Sawyer's.

Her head snapped up when she heard what sounded like footsteps.

Was someone there?

Sawyer?

No, if it was Sawyer, he would have told her he was coming.

Was she imaging things?

She was stressed out to the max right now, her shaking intensified, her heart was thumping, her pulse was drumming, and she wanted Sawyer here now.

What was that?

Her gaze snapped to a nearby tree.

Was something there?

It looked like a person, but she wasn't sure, and the more she looked the less she saw.

Her mind was probably just playing tricks on her.

Yes.

That was all it was.

"Keep telling yourself that," she muttered aloud because she needed to hear something that she was sure she was actually hearing.

The ankle she had rolled that created this mess throbbed. So far nothing else was hurting, but she knew that wasn't going to last. She was probably borderline going into shock, the psychological kind not the physical kind, and with adrenalin flooding her system it was masking the pain. But it would come. Later today she would be a mess, stiff and sore, and probably barely able to move.

How many minutes had it been since Sawyer left to come find her?

It felt like hours already.

Shouldn't he be here by now?

All he had to do was circle back down the hill on the path and then come along and find her.

It shouldn't take this long.

Had something happened to him?

What if there really was someone out there and they'd done something to Sawyer?

She was starting to panic.

Drawing enough air into her lungs was starting to become difficult.

Great.

Now she was hyperventilating.

Where was Sawyer?

She needed him.

Like right now.

There.

Right there.

That was someone walking toward her.

Ashley didn't think, she just staggered to her feet and ran, hoping she was going in the right direction. She didn't know if Sawyer had continued forward down the hill then doubled back for her, or doubled back down the path the way they'd come before looking for her.

She couldn't move very fast with her bad ankle, but she didn't care, she just had to get out of here.

Her ears strained as she ran, trying to listen out for the sounds of footsteps following her but her breathing was so labored it was all she could hear.

What was she doing?

Where was she going?

Everything was so jumbled in her head, it was like rolling down the hill had spun every single part of her about, and now her brain couldn't focus, and her body felt flimsy and wobbly.

But she didn't stop.

She couldn't.

If someone really was after her then she couldn't just stand there and wait for them to get her.

"Ah." Her foot caught on something, and she fell, landing hard on her hands, pain shooting up through her arms all the way to her shoulders.

Ashley felt like she was in a horror movie. Who fell over when they were running? She was clumsy, there was no doubt about it, she was never going to be a dancer, or a gymnast, or a figure skater or anything that required grace and balance, but she didn't fall over when she ran. She wasn't *that* clumsy.

She tried to get up, but her hands slipped on the cold, icy ground and she landed flat on her face.

What was wrong with her?

She was acting so goofy.

Tears streamed down her cheeks, the cold making them sting like little drops of fire. She tried to use that as motivation to get back on her feet because if she didn't, and there was someone after her, when they caught her she would feel a lot worse pain than just little stinging dots on her cheek.

Choking back a sob, she managed to get her feet beneath her and start running again.

The wind was picking up, and it buffeted against her. She felt so fragile, and that was something she hadn't felt since she was lying in a hospital bed, unable to talk, barely able to breathe, trying to process everything that had happened to her.

The only thing that had got her through that was Sawyer.

He had been there for her every step of the way.

Now she needed him and he wasn't here.

She wanted to break down and cry and sob and curl up in a little ball and just give up, but she didn't do that.

She never did that.

She would *never* do that.

It wasn't who she was.

She wouldn't give up.

She couldn't.

Because if she let herself fall apart then she was terrified that she would never be able to put herself back together again.

So she didn't give up, she just ran and kept on running, she ignored her ankle that beat a steady drum of pain with every step she took, the pain in the rest of her body was starting to make itself known. Her head hurt, and her back, her chest and stomach, her arms and legs, she wasn't sure there was a single part of her that didn't.

But she didn't stop.

She kept running.

She ran straight into someone and screamed.

∾

5:42 A.M.

. . .

"Ashley." Sawyer wrapped his hands around her biceps, so she didn't bounce straight back off him.

She was screaming.

It was like she didn't know he was here.

"Ash, stop screaming. Ashley, it's me, it's Sawyer." He gave her a gentle shake, not wanting to hurt her since he didn't know how badly she had injured herself falling down the hill, he just wanted to snap her out of this daze she appeared to be stuck in.

She was struggling in his grip, trying to get away from him, and he had no idea why.

It had only been a few minutes since she fell down the side of the hill. What could have happened that had freaked her out this much?

Was she more seriously hurt than she'd said?

Head injury perhaps?

Instead of holding her at arm's length, Sawyer drew her closer and held her tightly against his chest, one hand stroking her long hair in the hopes of calming her down a little.

Instead of raising his voice, he lowered it. "Ash, it's Sawyer. Calm down. I'm right here. I'm right here," he said again.

Slowly her struggles ceased until she was perfectly still in his embrace. "Sawyer?"

"Right here. What's going on? What happened? What freaked you out?"

Ashley might have stopped fighting him, but she hadn't really calmed down, she was hyperventilating and shaking like a leaf in his arms.

Her hysteria was starting to make him anxious.

What was going on?

It was clear something had upset her because when she'd called out to tell him where she was and what had happened she'd sounded a little breathless and like she was in pain, but she hadn't been scared. Now she was a freaked out mess.

"Honey." He pulled her back and bent his knees so he could look her in the eye. "You have to calm down. Now. Just breathe. Slow it down," he said when she continued to suck in air in short, sharp gasps. "In and out, in and out. There we go," he encouraged when she started breathing a little easier. "Now, tell me what upset you."

"Th-there was s-someone," she stammered.

"What someone? Where?" he asked, scanning the dark park.

"I h-heard footsteps, and I th-thought I s-saw someone."

If it wasn't for the tears streaming down her cheeks, the constant trembling, the hyperventilating, and the fact that she was clearly in full-on panic mode he would have thought she had imagined the whole thing. It was dark, there was someone who wanted her dead, she had taken a bad fall, it made sense that she had seen things that weren't there.

But Ashley didn't freak out like this.

The last three months she'd maybe cried four or five times, she hadn't had panic attacks, she'd had trouble sleeping, but that was about it, she had held it together amazingly well, for her to be this upset there had to be a reason. A good one.

"Are you sure?" he asked.

"I, um, no, I'm not sure," she said, "but I'm *pretty* sure. I heard what sounded like footsteps, I thought it was you but it wasn't. And then I thought I saw someone hiding behind a tree. I started running, and I thought someone was following me, but I don't know. I don't know," she finished, looking up at him helplessly.

She had been running like she was running for her life when she had crashed into him, she wouldn't have been running like that for no reason. If someone was watching her it could have been the serial killer who wanted her dead or it could have been someone else.

"Stay here, and I'll go look around," he told Ashley, if there was someone here then they had no doubt fled when they'd heard his and Ashley's voices, but it was worth checking out anyway.

"No," Ashley exclaimed, wrapping her arms around his waist and clinging to him like a terrified child. "Don't leave me."

"Ash, it's all right, calm down." He'd never seen her like this before, and it was freaking him out. "If someone is here I need to find out."

"I'm scared," Ashley whimpered, pressing herself closer.

"All right, then stay behind me," he said, pulling out his gun.

"Let's just go," she pleaded.

"We can't. What if it's the man who's after you? If he's still around here then I'm going to get him." There was no way he was walking away if there was any chance at all that the man was here. He wanted this over for Ashley, and he wasn't going to give up an opportunity to do that.

"Sawyer," she begged.

"It'll be fine," he said, already snapped into full-on bodyguard mode. His job was to protect Ashley and neutralize any threats that presented themselves. Maneuvering Ashley so she was behind him, he kept one arm on her, and slowly searched the surrounding area.

There was no one there.

There might have been earlier, but if someone had been after Ashley —either the killer or someone else—it made sense they would have split when they realized there were two people here.

"I'm sorry," Ashley murmured, sounding tired now.

"Don't be sorry, just because we didn't find him doesn't mean he wasn't here. When we get back to the house I'll call this in and have someone come and check out the whole area."

Right now his priority was getting Ashley back to his place. She was hurt, he still didn't know how badly, and he wasn't comfortable with her being here, it was too exposed. For all he knew, the killer had found them here at the park and had made an attempt to get Ashley, and was still here, waiting to make another attempt.

"Are you okay?" Sawyer turned his attention back to Ashley.

"Yeah." She nodded, drawing in a deep breath. She was obviously trying to collect herself and pull herself back together.

"Can you make it back to my place or should I call an ambulance?"

"I don't need an ambulance," she said quickly, which was only half an answer.

"Can you make the walk back home?"

"I think so," Ashley replied but didn't sound particularly sure. "I hurt my ankle, rolled it on something, that's why I fell."

She'd told him that before when she'd called up from the bottom of the hill. His heart still hadn't stopped racing. For a moment he'd thought that the killer had gotten her. When he'd heard her scream and then reached the top of the hill and seen no sign of her, he'd thought he had failed her, he had never been so scared in his life. Bringing her here had been a mistake, there would be no more early morning jogs at the park.

From the way she was standing, balancing her weight on one leg, he didn't think she could make the walk back to his house. She'd rolled the ankle, causing her to fall, then when she'd thought someone was there she'd run on it when she should have been resting it, probably making the ankle worse.

"Let's get you home," he said, picking her up.

"I can probably walk," she protested, but her arm curled around his shoulder.

"I'm sure you could, but I'd like to get home before lunchtime," he teased gently as he started walking toward his house.

"I beat you up the hill, didn't I?" she shot back.

Sawyer felt himself relax as Ashley relaxed. Seeing her so worked up got him worked up, neither of them had really slept last night, and the stresses of the last fifteen minutes had taken their toll on them both. When they got back to his place he'd call Jett and Morgan and have them check out the park and then come and speak with Ashley in case she had actually seen someone following her. He would also call Brian Xander, the doctor who worked for the same firm he did, and have him come and check Ashley over. After being attacked by a man in doctor's scrubs at the hospital, Ashley had been nervous about having any unknown medical person look after her, so Brian had been the one who had monitored her progress. He knew that having someone she trusted looking after her today would make her feel more comfortable.

Then once she had been looked at and interviewed she was going to go to bed and get some sleep. And maybe once he knew she was okay and getting some rest, he might be able to as well.

As much as Ashley needed to know she was safe, he needed to know she was safe too. The toll of the killer being out there was beginning to show in both of them. They both needed closure. Even if he and Ashley were never going to be more than friends he wanted to see her live well into old age, even if that meant she fell in love with someone else.

Sawyer clutched Ashley a little tighter and thanked his lucky stars that for now at least she was safe, and vowed to do whatever was necessary to make sure she remained so.

∼

6:00 A.M.

The bouncy motion of being carried in Sawyer's arms was making her feel sleepy.

Ashley hadn't slept well last night, even with the added comfort of knowing that Sawyer was just a couple of feet away in his bed. Now it was six in the morning, and she was utterly exhausted, if she lay down now she was pretty sure she'd be out for the rest of the day.

"Home sweet home," Sawyer announced as he opened the door and stepped inside.

As the warmth of the house washed over her, the pain hit.

It touched every part of her body.

Obviously the cold had been masking it, but now that she was out of it the pain wanted to make itself known.

"There you go." Sawyer set her down on the sofa. "You're still shaking, I'll go grab a blanket."

Ashley slowly eased herself back so her head rested on the cushions, and closed her eyes. It was nice to be out of the wind and cold even if it did make all her bumps and bruises ache.

"You look worse in the light," Sawyer murmured as he spread a blanket over her. "I've called Brian, he's on his way. Jett and Morgan are going to come too, and they've sent someone to the park as well. If someone was there they'll find out."

She felt silly now.

Like she had overreacted and caused all this drama over nothing.

There probably hadn't been anyone there, it was just her overactive imagination playing tricks on her.

"I'm sorry," she said in a small voice.

"Stop saying that. If you thought you were being followed of course you should say something," Sawyer told her, but she felt like he was just saying it to make her feel better. She had caused all this drama, and it might have been for nothing.

She had never fallen apart like that before.

Now she felt embarrassed, she didn't want Sawyer to see her like she'd been at the park, all hyperventilating and hysterical. She wished she could take the last half hour back and make it so it never existed.

"Look at you. You are a hot mess."

"My mom used to call me that," she said with a small reminiscent smile.

"She did?"

"Uh-huh. She used to say it to me all the time."

Her parents had been in their mid-forties when they conceived her naturally. After close to two decades of trying to have a baby they were thrilled. Despite the risks to her and her mother, she had been carried to term and was born without any of the complications that babies of older moms could have.

Unfortunately, her mother had been diagnosed with breast cancer when Ashley was eight. She had gone into remission, but then the cancer had come back three years later. Again she had gone into remission but had been struck down by the disease again during Ashley's senior year of high school and had passed away just before she graduated.

It had dampened the fun of going off to college a little, but her dad had encouraged her to get out there and make the most of her life and enjoy every second of it because that's what her mom would have wanted.

So she had.

She had lived her life to make her mom proud.

But a second blow had come just two years later.

Her father, only in his mid-sixties, had had a massive heart attack driving to work one morning. The car had spun out of control and slammed into a fence. He had been killed instantly.

And in that moment she had been left all alone in the world.

Until she had built a different kind of family.

A family of friends, friends who had proven that they were there for her when she needed them.

Sawyer was the center of that new little family.

"Let's clean you up." Sawyer sat beside her and took hold of her chin. Tilting her face toward him, he began cleaning away the blood and dirt that streaked her skin. "This looks like it hurts."

"It does." She winced as he touched the lump on her forehead. "I think I hit it on a tree on the way down the hill."

"You're lucky you didn't knock yourself out."

She was.

If she had been knocked unconscious and there really had been someone out there then she would have been completely vulnerable to them, and Sawyer wouldn't have even known where she was.

"There, that's a little better," Sawyer said, setting down the damp cloth but not releasing his grip on her chin.

Ashley sucked in a breath as she got that same feeling she'd gotten yesterday in the bath when they'd been playing with the fake snow.

That same feeling where all she wanted in the world was to kiss him.

"Sorry for falling apart earlier," she murmured. She didn't want that to change how he saw her. She had always been so strong, through her mother's illnesses and death, through her father's death, through everything that had happened nearly four months ago, she didn't want Sawyer to see her as weak now.

"Ash, there's someone out there that wants to kill you, you've had to give up your life, but it has never broken you. You have held up better than anyone else would have. It's okay to let the stress show sometimes, you don't have to hold it all inside. You are without a doubt the strongest person I know."

Sawyer's words warmed her from the inside, finally stilling the tremors that had been coursing through her body ever since her fall.

Subconsciously, her lips parted, and her tongue darted out to wet them.

Her gaze dropped to Sawyer's lips and then rose to meet his eyes.

They were so blue and so bright, and the urge to kiss him intensified.

His head dipped towards hers, hers moved toward his, and then just like it had yesterday, the doorbell rang.

"That must be Brian," Sawyer said, quickly standing.

"Yeah, must be," she echoed, disappointed. That was twice now she had wanted to kiss Sawyer, and twice that she thought he wanted to kiss her too, but both times they had been interrupted. Maybe that was a sign.

"Hey, Ashley, how are you doing?" Brian asked, sitting down beside her.

"Hey, Brian, thanks for coming." She forced herself to smile because she knew he had probably gotten out of bed to come here and check her out.

"No problem." He smiled. "So tell me what you hurt. I see scratches and what looks like a nasty bump on your head. What else?"

"I rolled my ankle right before I fell."

"You seem to be pretty lucid so I don't think you have a concussion, but that cut might need a few stitches. Let's take a look at your ankle." Brian lifted her leg, pulled off her sneaker, and then her sock. When he rolled up her sweatpants she could see that her ankle was already swollen and turning black and blue. Brian moved it from side to side and up and down, she winced with each movement. "How's that?"

"It hurts but it's not so bad," she replied.

"I don't think it's broken, but if you want we can go to the hospital to get it x-rayed."

"No," she said immediately. She didn't want to go anywhere, this was where she felt safe, and she didn't want to leave.

"Keep it iced and elevated for the rest of the day, try to stay off it as much as you can. What else?"

"I think everything else is just bumps and bruises, I'm sore all over but nothing is too bad."

"Let's give you a look over then." Brian's hands skimmed her body, probing and prodding any time she winced. "I think you're right," he pronounced. "Bumps and bruises, a sprained ankle, and the gash on your head that I'm going to put a couple of stitches in."

That was what she had been expecting to hear, but it was nice to have a doctor confirm it.

Brian put two stitches in her head. "There. I'm going to leave you some painkillers and some sedatives so you can get some rest later."

Usually she didn't take sedatives, she didn't like the groggy feeling you got the next day, but she was exhausted but wired, and taking them might be the only way she could get any sleep.

"Hi, Ashley," Jett said as he and Morgan joined them in the living room.

"Hey." She tried to muster a smile for the FBI agents, but she was feeling worn out.

"I'll head off, let you guys do your thing," Brian announced. "Ash, call if you need anything or you feel worse, okay? And, Sawyer, if you notice any changes in her mental state take her straight to the hospital."

"We will," Sawyer answered for her.

"I don't really know what to tell you," she told the agents once Brian was gone. "Like I told Sawyer, I'm not positive that anyone was there." Ashley was feeling like such an idiot over what happened at the park.

"That's okay." Morgan smiled and sat beside her. "Why don't you just tell us what you remember and we'll take it from there."

"It was probably nothing," she cautioned again.

"But we're talking about your life so we're not taking any chances. If it's nothing, no big deal, we check out the park and move on, no harm done," Jett told her.

Since it appeared they weren't leaving until she told them what had happened, she may as well get it over with. "Sawyer and I were jogging, and I wanted to beat him up the hill. I did, but when I turned around to tease him about it, I must have stepped on a rock or something. My ankle rolled and gave out and I fell down the hill. When I heard Sawyer calling my name I told him what happened and he circled back around to come get me. I was waiting, and I heard what I thought was footsteps. I thought it was Sawyer, but he didn't say anything. Then I thought I saw someone. I wasn't sure, it was dark, but then I thought someone was coming toward me and I ran."

Ashley kind of held her breath as she awaited their response, expecting to be told she'd taken a fall, hit her head, she'd been under a lot of stress lately, and she had probably just imagined the whole thing.

Instead, Jett looked thoughtful. "The figure you saw was it small like maybe it was just a stray dog or something, or was it the size of a person?"

She thought then said, "It was the size of a person."

"Child, woman, or man-size?" Morgan asked.

"Man-size," she replied.

"I know it was dark, but could you recognize anything about him?" Jett asked.

"No, I'm sorry. You don't just think I'm crazy?" she asked tentatively.

"No, of course not. As soon as it's light we're going to check out the park, see if ERT can find any footprints or anything. If there was someone there it might have been the man after you, or someone else up to no good, it could have been a jogger with earphones in who just didn't know you were there, or it could have been a homeless person. We'll figure this out, I don't want you to stress over it. And to be safe I think Michael or Brady are going to hang around today, just in case it was the killer we're looking for and he followed you back here," Jett explained.

She hadn't thought about the possibility of the man in the park following them, but now that they'd brought it up she was relieved to know that either Brady or Michael, who was another bodyguard and friend who worked at the firm, were going to be watching over her as well.

For now though she'd had enough, she'd told them all she knew, and now she needed to go lie down.

"I think I'm going to go get some sleep," she announced.

"You should stay here, don't walk up the stairs on your ankle. We'll go talk in the other room," Sawyer said.

"Yeah, okay," she agreed.

"Here you go." He handed her the pills Brian had left for her.

Ashley didn't think twice, just swallowed the pain pill and the sedative, then Sawyer helped her lie down and tucked the blanket around her.

"Call out if you need anything, okay?"

"Okay," she said, snuggling down into the soft, fluffy couch cushions. She didn't even remember the others leaving the room, her exhausted body and mind gave out, and she floated off to sleep.

~

1:19 P.M.

He sat watching her sleep.

Sawyer could do it for hours.

He *had* been doing it for hours.

Ever since Jett and Morgan had left he'd been sitting in an armchair beside the couch where Ashley was sprawled out, still fast asleep. He had thought of heading upstairs and getting some sleep himself, but he didn't want to leave her alone. He hadn't even been able to go to the kitchen to get something to eat, or to go and grab a book, he just wanted to sit here and watch her.

Okay, so that was a little creepy stalker-like, but he didn't care. Sawyer knew that sooner or later this killer would be caught and then Ashley would be gone. He knew it was what was best for her, two almost-kisses aside, she didn't love him the way he loved her so what kind of relationship could they ever have?

As much as he would have loved to have kissed her either time—or both times—it had almost happened it was probably for the best that they hadn't. It made it easier to move on. If they'd kissed then he'd know exactly what he was missing.

Who was he kidding?

He knew what he was missing.

His phone buzzed, and he pulled it out of his pocket.

It was a text from his sister saying she was at the front door but didn't want to knock or ring the bell in case Ashley was sleeping.

As quietly as he could he stood and crossed to the door, opening it to find Savannah standing there, looking pale.

"You okay?" he asked as he took her arm and led her inside.

"Just been feeling a little sick the last few days," Savannah replied.

"Let's go through to the kitchen," he said quietly, nodding his head at Ashley.

Savannah nodded and followed him through the living room and into the kitchen diner. He knew what was bothering his sister and he hoped he could convince her to let it go.

"You want something to eat?" he asked. He was hungry, and since he'd already left Ashley's side he may as well grab something to eat.

"I'm not really hungry," Savannah said, sliding into a chair at the table.

"Right because you're "sick"," he said, doing air quotes.

Savannah glared at him. "Why are you mocking me for being sick?"

"I'm not mocking you, I believe that you haven't been feeling well, but I think we both know that you aren't sick." He grabbed ham and cheese from the fridge and a couple of slices of bread.

"What am I then?"

"You already know the answer to that. Why are you fighting it?" He didn't understand what was going on with her. She had never been one to back away from anything, she'd had to learn to walk again twice after her injuries, she was tough, and he knew she wanted this. So why was she trying to run away from it?

His sister shrugged restlessly.

"Sav." He stopped making his sandwich and came and sat with her at the table. "What's going on? You want this. You've wanted it for the last year. I remember you last Christmas, you and Jett had just gotten back together, and you were going all gooey over Tom and Hannah's little baby. Now you and Jett are married, you're happy, you both want kids, now you're probably pregnant, and you're trying to pretend that you aren't. Why?"

"I'm scared," Savannah whispered.

"Of what?"

"Of being pregnant, of not being pregnant, of bringing a baby into a world where there are so many evil people, of never being able to have a baby, of something happening to the baby, of something happening to me, of something happening to Jett," Savannah said in a rush.

Wow.

She was really freaking out.

That was so unlike his sister. Savannah usually ran straight toward trouble if someone needed help, but she didn't usually invent trouble where there wasn't any.

"Don't you think maybe you're just emotional because you're pregnant?" he asked. "All of those are valid concerns. There are evil people in the world, there is always a chance that something could happen to you or Jett, or the baby, but it's not like you to be scared about it."

"I was so excited, but then in February I was late, and we thought I might be pregnant, but I wasn't. And then the same thing happened in July. Then everything that's been going on with Ashley, and I don't know why, I'm just scared. I just don't know if I'm more scared that I am pregnant or that I'm not."

"Pregnancy hormones," he said. "You need to take a pregnancy test. You're working yourself up about it instead of just doing it. You've been sick for a couple of days now, this time I think you're really pregnant. When you leave here you go buy yourself a pregnancy test and you take it today."

"Yeah, you're right, I think I'm working myself up because I don't have an answer one way or the other. I'll take the test. Thanks, Sawyer." She smiled at him.

"Of course. That's what I'm here for, right?" He and Savannah were always open and honest with one another, they told it like it was, no sugarcoating. Neither of them ever took offense because they were family, twins, they had always been a big part of each other's lives, there wasn't anyone he was closer to than his sister.

"Now it's time for you to take your own advice," Savannah said.

"About what?" he asked, although he already knew what she was talking about.

"Ashley."

"What about her?"

"Sawyer." Savannah rolled her eyes at him.

"Okay," he sighed, "but my situation with Ashley is not the same as you being scared of being pregnant."

"It's not different," his sister contradicted. "I'm scared about having a baby after losing Dad when we were kids and then everything that's happened to me over the last few years, and you're afraid to tell Ashley how you feel about her."

"It is different," Sawyer insisted. "Because underneath your fear you're excited."

"And you wouldn't be excited if you told Ashley you've been in love with her for the last couple of years and she said she felt the same way?"

Of course he would.

The problem was, that wasn't going to happen.

"I was scared to let Jett back in after he hurt me," Savannah admitted. "When he wasn't there for me when I needed him it hurt so badly. So deeply. Like the pain had sliced inside me and cut away at my insides. I thought I could never trust him again, and I was afraid that I'd be hurt again if I put myself out there. So I didn't. I told him to go, and he did. When he came back I was still too afraid to even listen to him explain why he hadn't been able to be there for me. So I shut him out. I hid behind my anger. I wouldn't even listen to him. But you told me I should, and Chloe told me I should, she said that I didn't have to take him back, but I should at least listen and then make a decision with all the facts. I almost blew that too, but I didn't, I took a step back, tried to set my emotions aside, and look at things objectively, and when I did there was only one important thing that stood out at me. I loved Jett. Everything else could be dealt with."

Savannah made it sound so simple.

But it wasn't simple.

Emotions and relationships rarely were.

"You're afraid to tell her because she might not feel the same way, but if you told her and she said she didn't feel the same what's the worst thing that could happen?"

"I'd lose my best friend." If Ashley didn't feel the same way he did—and Sawyer didn't believe that she did—then things could never go back to the way they were now. They would both be way too self-conscious, her because she didn't reciprocate his feelings, and him because he had put the elephant in the room.

"But in trying not to lose your best friend, which is only conjecture because you don't know that would happen, you might be missing out on getting the love of your life. Is that the trade-off you want to make?"

He hadn't thought of it like that before.

He had only ever looked at the situation as what he would lose if he told Ashley how he felt. He'd never looked at it at what he might gain by telling her.

"Face our fears," Savannah said quietly. "That's what we always used to tell each other. When I was afraid of the dark, when you were afraid to jump off the diving board at the pool, when I was afraid to learn to drive because of the accident, when you were afraid to get your appendix out, we faced all those things because Watsons are tough, and they don't run away from the things that scare them, they face them. So I'll go home and take a pregnancy test, and you go for it and talk to Ashley, tell her how you feel, deal?" She held out her hand.

It wouldn't be easy, and he would have to be prepared for her to reject him. And not just reject him but move out and ask someone else to take over as her bodyguard. Their friendship could be over, or he could get everything he'd ever dreamed about.

Sawyer shook his sister's hand. "Deal."

～

7:40 P.M.

He was excited.

Nothing beat going out hunting for another girl.

It was a little harder in the winter than it was in the summer to find one. People didn't stay out as long when the weather was cold and it got dark early. Although it was Christmas time and people were out celebrating, having dinners, and catching up with family and friends, there weren't that many of them wandering around on their own.

The other night he had been lucky, but tonight he was worried that he would have to go back home empty-handed.

He didn't want to, and it would definitely be a huge disappointment, but he'd rather play things safe and go home without having taken a life, than he would do something risky that ended up getting him caught and sent to prison.

He wondered how long he could go on like this. How long could he remain one step ahead of the cops? How long could he keep getting away with what he was doing?

He hoped indefinitely, but there was no way to know for sure so he had to make the most of every single kill he made because he never knew when it would be his last.

How he was going to cope when that time came he didn't know.

Killing had become his purpose for living, feeding that beast inside him, it was now as important to him as eating, as breathing. He *needed* to do it, if he didn't, he thought the chances of him imploding were very real.

He had done everything his therapist had recommended, but nothing had given him the peace of mind that killing had.

It was weird; he thought that taking lives had actually saved his own.

Irony.

It was definitely ironic.

He caught sight of a pretty dark-haired young woman leaving a restaurant. She was with a group of about ten, men and women, a teenager, and two pre-teens. He expected her to walk away with at least one of the people, but after they said their goodbyes, hugging and kissing each other, the young woman waved and headed off in the opposite direction.

Perfect.

It looked like his luck was holding after all.

He put his phone, that he was pretending to talk into, in his pocket and followed along after the woman. He knew this area from top to bottom, he knew every alley, every store, every single inch of it. After following the woman for barely a minute he knew where she was heading, the parking lot down the restaurant district's south end.

The woman was distracted, looking at the Christmas wreaths hanging on all the doors and the fairy lights strung up and down all the trees that lined the streets, so she didn't notice when he brushed past her and walked off, speeding his stride up a little so that he could get to the alley.

When he reached it he ducked in, deliberately not trying to hide what he was doing. Should anyone notice him and they saw him trying to slink in like he was up to no good then he would stick in someone's memory. However, if he walked in purposefully like he had a reason to be there then no one would give him a second glance.

He had to make sure he was in the alley enough that she wouldn't see him as she came along, but not so far in that he couldn't grab her as she passed him by.

Details.

It was all about these little details.

Mess up just one little thing and his whole world could come crashing down around him.

Positioning himself in just the right spot, he waited anxiously, nervous excitement bubbling in his stomach. He knew it made him a bad person to get so much pleasure from ending another human being's life, but he didn't care. It was fun, there was no point in denying it.

There she was.

As she stepped into view it was like time slowed down and he entered a parallel world. This was the way it always was. From the second he wrapped his arm around a woman and yanked her away from the rest of the world and into his until the second their life slipped away, it always felt like hours rather than the few minutes it was in reality.

He darted out and grabbed hold of her, dragging her up against his body and then moving them both away from the prying eyes of those on the street and into the quiet alley.

They were always stunned for the first couple of moments, then the fog cleared and their brains snapped back into focus, and their fight or flight instinct kicked in. Since he'd taken the flight option out of the equation by holding them pinned against his chest, they had no choice but to go with fight. All but a couple of them had fought like caged animals to get away from him. He liked that, you should always have that fight inside you.

He was always prepared for them to start fighting him so he moved quickly. So long as he kept moving and didn't stop to give them a chance to get one up on him, things usually seemed to flow smoothly.

The rope was already in his free hand, and he wrapped it quickly around her neck, not enough to do any real damage but enough so that it took her focus away from him and to the rope as she clawed at it. With her distracted, he slammed her up against the wall, the blow was always enough to stun them, and while he kept the rope tight but not too tight around her neck, cutting off just enough of her air supply to keep her dazed, with his other he unzipped her pants and then his own.

He never had to worry about being in the mood, just knowing what was coming had him ready the second he stepped foot in the alley. He shoved inside her, and in less than a minute he came in a fiery burst of ecstasy that was the most addictive feeling on the planet.

As always it was over too soon.

He pulled out, zipped up, and then shoved the woman down to the ground.

However pathetically, she was still fighting him, and as he tightened the rope, one of her fingernails gouged into his hand, taking out a chunk of flesh. He would have to make sure he cleaned that thoroughly when he was finished, he didn't want the FBI to get his DNA.

He watched her eyes as the lack of oxygen began to affect her. Her movements grew sluggish, and her eyes started to grow cloudy.

Before he had taken a life he had never thought of eyes as cloudy. But they were. As a kid he had loved lying on the grass, staring up at the sky, watching the clouds float across the blue expanse, trying to see what he could find in the shapes of the clouds. It was like that with eyes, only instead of looking for shapes he looked for emotions. There was anger and fear, disbelief and sorrow, shock and acceptance, and then right at the end there was a look he couldn't describe. It was like they had passed into the next world a beat before their heart stopped and they saw what lay there.

He had always wondered what lay beyond this life. He knew that he would find out one day, but he wished someone could give him a clue now.

He tightened the rope again, pulling it as tightly as he could and watched as it pressed down into the skin. It would leave a mark, and he liked that, it was like these women would take a piece of him with them into eternity and that piece would be with them forever.

Just before it was over he leaned in close and whispered, "Thank you."

It was important to him that he always thanked them for the sacrifice they had made. They had died so that he could live, so the beast inside him could be temporarily satiated.

To be safe he kept the rope around her neck for a full minute longer than was necessary, then he removed it and touched his fingers to her throat, his cheek was above her mouth, and his other hand on her chest. When he felt no pulse, no puff of air on his cheek, and his hand didn't rise and fall with her chest, he was satisfied that she was really dead.

Another one dead.

A calm settled over him, peace started in his stomach and spread out to consume him.

The calm wasn't lasting as long as it had at first. In the beginning, he could go months before the beast needed another life, now he had just killed, and that need was already hovering at the edges of his consciousness.

He didn't let it ruin his night.

The beautiful woman beneath him was proof of what a good night it had been.

Riding the high he cleaned up, and strode out of the alley, off to enjoy the rest of his evening, content in the knowledge he could make another kill soon, and that one day it would be Ashley Fallon's dead body lying beneath him.

∾

8:56 P.M.

"How is it this cold?"

Jett looked up as Morgan joined him in the alley. His partner was rugged up like she'd been dropped in the middle of the Arctic Circle. "It's going to get a lot colder once the snow comes."

"I know." Morgan looked so devastated that Jett couldn't help but laugh.

"How have you made it to twenty-seven," he snickered.

"I have no idea. I really need to win the lottery and buy my own tropical island so I never have to live through another freezing winter again." Morgan sobered and rubbed her gloved hands together. "What's her name?"

"This is Brynn Bowe," Jett said, looking back down at the young woman who had lost her life just an hour or two ago.

"How did this get called in so quickly?"

"Just a fluke. One of the stores that backs onto the alley, the owner came back because he thought he accidentally threw something in the dumpster, I can't remember what he said it was, but he came back here and found her."

If the man had come back just an hour or so earlier he would either have interrupted the killer and saved Brynn's life or gotten himself killed. Given that the killer seemed to put self-preservation before anything else as evidenced by the fact that he ran when the cops arrived at the scene of Ashley's near murder, and that he had chosen to run rather than take on Sawyer at the hospital when he came after Ashley the second time. Jett believed that if the store owner had shown up then the killer would have run and Brynn might have survived.

But like he had learned in his own life, you couldn't undo things and do them over the way you wished you had done them the first time. Playing the should've, would've, could've game only drove you crazy.

If he could, he would take back letting Savannah down, which had broken her trust in him and resulted in them losing years that they could have been together enjoying each other. As much as he wished that hadn't happened he had to focus on the fact that they were together now, and if he could just convince Savannah to take the test to confirm it, they were expecting their first baby.

His life was as close to perfect as possible, but this case was weighing him down. It hovered in the back of his mind almost constantly, and he'd lost count of the number of nights he had dreamed about it.

Every time another victim fell that weight got heavier and he was worried that if they never found this guy then eventually that weight would end up crushing the joy out of his life.

"You okay, Jett?"

He blinked and looked over to find Morgan watching him closely, a concerned look in her pretty green eyes. "I'm okay, it's just this case is ..." He dropped his gaze back to Brynn's lifeless body discarded in an alley like trash. "This case is just getting to me."

"Three years is a long time to be chasing one killer."

"Every death I take personally, eighteen young women dead, almost nineteen, because I couldn't find him. I still can't find him. We don't even have a direction to move in. We're no closer to catching him than we were when Blake and I first got this case. How many more women are going to die?"

"He'll mess up eventually," Morgan said, trying to console him.

"He hasn't so far. Three years, eighteen dead, and not a single slip up."

"But he's already starting to devolve," his partner reminded him. "Less time between kills, this was only forty-eight hours this time, he's already started the downward spiral. The further down he goes the quicker he's going to start looking for victims, and the quicker he moves the sloppier he'll get. He *will* make a mistake eventually and then we'll have him."

She was right, Jett knew that, their killer was devolving and sooner or later he would make a mistake, and sooner or later they would get him, but he wanted it sooner rather than later. He didn't want another woman to lose her life because he couldn't do his job, and he certainly didn't want Ashley to lose her life.

"If we don't get him before he gets Ash..." Jett trailed off, unable to finish the sentence. He knew what Ashley meant to Sawyer, and Sawyer was family, he was Savannah's twin brother, and they had gotten to be really good friends over the last year. He knew what it was like to fear for the life of the woman you loved and he didn't want Sawyer to keep living with that hovering over him.

"We will."

"We don't know that." He wanted it to be true, but there were no guarantees in life.

"He doesn't know where she is," Morgan reminded him. "If he did he would have already tried to get to her. He wouldn't be able to wait. He couldn't even wait that first day, he went after her in the hospital just hours after trying to kill her the first time. After waiting nearly four months for a chance to get to her if he knew that she was at Sawyer's, he would have gone there already."

"We don't know that," he said again. "ERT checked out the park where Ashley fell, she was right, she wasn't imagining things, someone *was* there." He and Morgan hadn't been convinced that Ashley's claim someone had been there was true. Not that they'd thought she was lying, but she'd been under a lot of stress, and then she'd fallen and hit her head. It was plausible that she had just hallucinated the whole thing. But ERT had found three sets of footprints in the area. A smaller set that was Ashley's, a large set that were Sawyer's, and a set that were slightly smaller than Sawyer's that belonged to an unknown—but probably male—person.

"Someone, but we don't know who. What you told Ash was true, it could be anyone, a jogger with earphones in, a homeless person, some random criminal up to something, or our killer."

"Any reports of crimes in that park in the last few weeks? Sexual assaults, muggings, abductions, anything?"

"No," Morgan replied. "I looked into it, there's been nothing unusual or criminal at that park since the year before last."

"So it's not out of the question that it was some random guy, but if it was this killer then he would have found a way to follow her, and I think you're right, he would have made a move already."

"So we don't think this was related. Either some innocent misunderstanding or simply wrong place wrong time. This isn't a park near Ashley's house, and it's not a place she goes regularly, so I don't think the killer would have gone there in the hopes of finding her. I don't think this whole park thing is going to go anywhere. We don't have enough to go on. We might be able to find some of the people who were there this morning, but it was dark and cold, and I doubt anyone saw anything useful anyway. I think we're just going to have to—"

"Hey, guys," one of the crime scene techs working the scene called out. Jett knew the woman, she worked with Savannah who also worked for the FBI's evidence response team.

"Did you find something?" Morgan asked.

"I was bagging her hands, and there's something under one of her nails, I think we might be able to get DNA." The woman was stumbling over her words she was speaking so quickly as she beamed with excitement.

DNA.

That they might have this guy's DNA seemed too good to be true.

Jett almost didn't want to believe it.

He didn't want to get his hopes up.

Just because they had—or might have—the killer's DNA didn't

mean that it would lead them anywhere, they still had to run it through the system and match it to someone.

But they were making progress.

They actually had something.

After three long years they had something.

"What did I tell you." Morgan was beaming at him, practically vibrating with enthusiasm. "I told you as he picked up the pace and started killing too quickly that he would slip up and make a mistake, and he did. He rushed through his clean up routine, and he left something behind."

"Let's hope he's in the system, if he is we could be bringing him into custody in just a few hours," Jett said. Maybe Ashley and Sawyer would get their Christmas miracle this year like he and Savannah had last Christmas.

∾

10:27 P.M.

Savannah felt like she was sitting on hot coals.

She couldn't stay still, she kept squirming and wriggling and had read the same page in her book at least ten times, and she still had no idea what it said. She could barely even remember which book she was reading, who the characters were, or what the storyline was.

Nor did she care.

She wanted Jett to come home.

He had texted her around eight to say he was just leaving and should be home soon, and then about five minutes later had texted again to say that he had to go to a crime scene.

The serial rapist and killer had struck again.

Another young woman was dead, another family ripped apart, and she hated it.

She knew how much this case had been weighing on Jett, and she knew how personally he was taking these murders. She hated seeing that, when he hurt she hurt, and she hated seeing him blaming himself for something that was outside of his control. They had been back together for a year now, and she knew how many hours he had put into this case. Hopefully they caught a break soon.

That wasn't the only reason she was on edge tonight.

Her deal with her brother was weighing on her mind.

She wanted to take the pregnancy test, and she didn't.

It was weird to feel two ways about something. She didn't usually. Usually she knew what she wanted, and she went and did it, but lately she felt so indecisive. She was terrified that she was pregnant, and she was terrified that she wasn't. Sawyer was right, she needed to stop with the worrying and just do it.

As soon as Jett got home she was going to take the test.

Savannah glanced at the clock on the wall for the hundredth time.

One minute had passed since she last looked.

Why was time moving so slowly tonight?

Headlights shone through the window and she bounced up.

Jett was home.

It was finally time.

She hurried as fast as she could with her cane to the door to meet Jett the second he walked through it.

"Whoa," he said as he threw the door open and almost walked straight into her. "I thought you'd be in bed. Are you feeling better?" His arm slipped around her waist and he drew her against his chest. She felt a deep breath shudder out of him and she knew that holding her helped him feel grounded when he felt so out of control with this case.

"I'm feeling better," she assured him, snuggling her head under his chin. Holding her might help ground Jett, but it helped ground her too. All her silly paranoia about being pregnant or not being pregnant melted away when she was in her husband's arms.

Fear wasn't a comfortable place for her. Not that she thought it was for anyone, but she knew what it was like to truly fear for your life and for the lives of people you cared about. That was probably playing into this panicking about having a baby. She so badly wanted to have a child with Jett, they both wanted a family, but making it a reality was a scary thing.

No more worrying though.

No more putting it off.

She was ready to take that test.

"Did you eat dinner already? Do you want to grab something before—"

"No," she interrupted.

"You want to go straight to bed?"

"Nope," she said, a small smile tugging at the corners of her mouth. It was funny after worrying about it the last couple of days she was actually excited about taking the test now. Her brother always knew the best way to motivate her, she loved that they were always so straightforward with each other, she hoped he was ready to take his own leap of faith as she took hers.

"What do you want to do then?"

"What you've wanted me to do for the last few days."

"Really?" He pulled back so he could see her.

"Really."

"What changed your mind? Not that I'm not thrilled, but up until now you've been adamant you just have the flu. Why are you now ready to accept that you're probably pregnant?"

"I talked to Sawyer."

Jett shook his head. "That brother of yours, too bad we can't bottle him up and pull him out when you need some sense talked into you."

Savannah giggled. "He doesn't do anything special, he just tells me to get over myself and stop being afraid. You always try to make me feel better, but I'm a tough-love kind of girl."

"I'll have to remember that next time you go all neurotic on me," he teased.

"Hey." She playfully punched him in the shoulder. "I don't get neurotic very often." The last time she'd been neurotic about something was last year when she'd been afraid to try walking again after the second injury to her hip. That time it had been Jett, not her brother, who'd helped her overcome her fears, so really it was a tie between the two men in her life.

"We'll blame it on the pregnancy hormones." Jett kissed her forehead. "You ready?"

"Ready," she said confidently, she really was ready.

"You want to go grab the test?"

"Got it." She pulled the stick out of her pocket.

"Then let's do this." He beamed at her, his green eyes twinkling.

Hand in hand they walked to the downstairs bathroom, she was bursting with excitement and now couldn't even remember why she hadn't wanted to do this earlier.

"Good luck." Jett kissed her.

She rolled her eyes. "We already know what the test is going to say."

"But we both need confirmation."

They did.

Breathing in deeply, she went into the bathroom and peed on the stick. Once she'd washed her hands she opened the door to find Jett pacing nervously.

Jump ahead eight months or so, and she could picture him pacing just like this while she was in labor.

"You kinda look good all nervous like that," Savannah said.

Jett glared at her. "I hate waiting."

"I know you do, you're so impatient." She smirked, egging him on.

"You know all about that don't you? You sure made me wait for you."

"And wasn't I worth it?"

He softened and stopped his pacing. "You were more than worth it and I would wait for you forever, there isn't anyone else in this world that I would wait for. Well, maybe this little one." He put his hand on her stomach.

It was weird to think that there might be a human being growing inside her.

She adored her friend Hannah's one-year-old daughter Noelle, and her best friend Chloe's one-year-old son Asher. They were so much fun and so sweet, she loved when they wrapped their chubby little arms around her neck and kissed her cheek.

Savannah felt her eyes misting over, one day soon it could be her own little son or daughter giving her hugs and kisses. It was amazing to think about.

"You're excited again," Jett said softly.

"As much as I was this time last year when we first talked about having kids. Sorry for being a mess the last few weeks." One tear trickled down her cheek, weaving a slow line down to her chin.

"Don't be sorry, if something freaks you out it is what it is, and becoming parents and being responsible for another human being that's a big thing. But you are going to be the most amazing mother," Jett said. The pad of his thumb brushed her chin and caught the tear.

"Thanks, I really needed to hear that. This little baby and I are so lucky to have you."

Jett leaned down and kissed her softly and sweetly. "I think it's time."

"You do it," she said, suddenly nervous, not that she was pregnant but that she might not be. Now that she had acknowledged her fears she was able to let them go and move past them. "Well?" she asked when Jett picked up the stick but didn't say anything.

She wasn't pregnant.

They'd both been wrong.

He just didn't know how to tell her.

"Jett? Would you say something please? If it's bad news just say it and get—" Her sentence was broken off when Jett crushed his mouth against hers and kissed her breathless.

"We're having a baby," Jett said, his grin so wide it was like his mouth was going to break.

"We are?" Savannah hardly dared to believe it.

"We are," he said, wrapping his hands around her waist and picking her up off the floor, spinning her around.

A baby.

They were having a baby.

Her gaze settled on the Christmas tree. Chloe always said that Christmas was a time for miracles, and although she had never believed it before with everything that had happened last year, getting this news she was definitely convinced that things happened at Christmas that couldn't happen at any other time of the year.

～

11:07 P.M.

. . .

She was still asleep. Ashley had been out ever since she'd taken the sleeping pill at around seven this morning. That she was still out sixteen hours later was a testament to how truly exhausted she was and how little sleep she had been getting lately.

Sawyer had dozed a little throughout the day. Knowing that Ashley was asleep, and that his friend and colleague Michael Stein was sitting in a car outside the house, had been enough to let his mind and body relax enough to get the rest he needed.

Since it was late, Sawyer was just debating picking Ashley up and carrying her upstairs to bed when she began to stir.

"Ash?"

"Mmm," came the mumbled reply as she blinked sleepily and tugged a hand out from under the blankets to rub her eyes. "What time is it? How long was I asleep?"

"It's a little after eleven, you've been sleeping for the last sixteen hours."

"Wow, I can't believe I slept the whole day away." Ashley pushed herself up into a sitting position, using her hands to steady herself.

"You were exhausted and needed the rest. How're you feeling?"

"Groggy. I hate this feeling, it's why I don't usually take sleeping pills."

"You needed the rest," he reminded her. "How are all your bumps and bruises?"

"Sore. I feel sore all over, but nothing hurts too badly." She gave him a small smile.

"How's your head?" Although Brian had said he didn't think Ashley had a concussion, she'd still hit her head so he still needed to make sure the injury wasn't more serious than they'd thought.

"It's okay, I have a small headache, but it's probably more from the pills than banging my head on the tree."

"And your ankle?"

Ashley narrowed her eyes at him. "It's sore but okay, *Dr.* Sawyer."

He poked his tongue out. "Just doing my job."

"I thought you were my bodyguard not my doctor," she retorted.

"Actually, speaking about that, I have news." He'd gotten a text from Jett a few hours ago telling him about the development in the case. He had debated waking Ashley to give her the news but decided it could wait, she really had needed the sleep.

"Bad news?" Ashley's face fell, her dark eyes miserable.

He would do anything to take away what had happened to her. If wishes were possible he would wish that none of this had ever happened. But he couldn't. What he could do was tell her that maybe there was an end in sight. "Bad and good."

"He killed someone else, didn't he?" Ashley asked, tears were already welling up in her eyes.

As much as he wanted to protect her from the truth, he knew it wasn't the right thing to do. Trying to keep her in the dark was only going to add to her anxiety because it would make her feel like she didn't have anything to hold onto. She needed to know what was happening, it kept her grounded. "He did."

She took a moment to absorb that. "That's two women in two days, he's devolving."

"It looks like it."

"He made a mistake?" she asked hopefully.

"He did."

"What did he do?"

"He didn't clean up properly after he killed a young woman tonight. It was called in not long after it happened because apparently the owner of one of the stores that backed into the alley came back for something. Jett and Morgan went to the scene, and ERT was there, when they went to bag the woman's hands they found skin under one of her nails. She scratched him, and he forgot to clean it properly."

"So there might be DNA." Ashley beamed and clapped her hands together, looking even more excited than she'd been about the fake snow yesterday.

"There *might* be," he said carefully, he wanted her to be excited, but he also wanted her to be realistic. "Hopefully there is, and ERT was pretty confident they would find something useful, but there are no guarantees that they'll get a hit on it. We might have his DNA, but that doesn't mean this is over. Yes when we find him this will prove he killed this woman, but that doesn't mean the DNA will lead us to him. It also doesn't mean that we'll be able to prove that he's the man who killed the first sixteen women or tried to kill you."

"What do you mean?" Ashley looked confused.

"He changed the weapon he used to strangle these last two women," he told her.

Her hands moved to touch her neck. She was wearing a scarf to cover her scars, he knew she was self-conscious about them, she'd never let him see them since those first couple of days in the hospital. Sawyer wasn't sure that she knew she did it but Ashley often compulsively touched her neck, her fingers would linger there like she almost needed the feel of the scars to remind her she was alive.

"Ash." He moved from the armchair to sit beside her on the couch. "I'm not trying to dampen your mood. This is great news. It really is. I hope they get a hit and this is over soon. And you saw him, you can identify him as the man who assaulted you, that should tie him to all the other murders. This is it, this is the beginning of the end. I don't know when the end will come, but it is coming."

Ashley's gaze moved to something behind him, the Christmas tree if he had to guess. "Christmas miracles," she murmured. "They'll get a hit, and they'll find him because it's Christmas time and that's what happens at Christmas, you get those things that you need. I *need* him to be caught. It's not a want, it's a need, I need him to not be out there anymore."

Sawyer slipped an arm around her shoulders and tugged on her so she rested against him. "If anyone deserved to get what they need this Christmas it's definitely you."

"I think we both deserve it," Ashley said, laying her head on his shoulder. "I know this has been rough on you too."

"Nothing compared to what you're going through," he said. This wasn't about him it was about Ashley, and he so badly wanted her to get her Christmas miracle and have the man who had hurt her so badly and caused her to live in fear for months to be in handcuffs—or a body bag —before the sun rose on Christmas morning.

"I love that you want to put me first, but this has been as hard on you as it has on me. I was on the phone with you when it happened, you saved my life twice, and then you gave up your life to let me come and live here with you. I can never tell you how thankful I am for everything you've done for me."

"That's what best friends are for," he reminded her.

"And I have the very best friend there ever was. So, what did you do today while I slept?" Ashley asked, sounding a little sleepy. When this was over he wouldn't be surprised if she slept for a week. Stress took a toll on your body, especially this level of stress.

"Not much, I got a little sleep myself, and Savannah came over for a while." Sawyer felt nervous butterflies take up residence in his stomach. He and his sister had a deal, he knew that she would follow through and now it was up to him to do the same thing.

"That's nice, I'm glad you weren't alone," Ashley said.

"It was nice. Actually Savannah and I talked about you a little. She wanted to know how you were doing, if you were hanging in there, and if there was anything she could do to help. Savannah has been scared to take a pregnancy test, and I encouraged her to set aside her fears and go for it. She also encouraged me to do the same." Sawyer dragged in a deep breath, it was now or never. "Ashley, there's something I need to tell you, I probably should have said it a long time ago, but I was afraid of losing you. Ash, I'm in love with you," he blurted out before he could lose his nerve.

He waited anxiously for her response but there wasn't one.

She didn't say anything.

Exactly what he had been afraid was going to happen looked like it was about to play out.

Then he heard soft little snores.

She was asleep.

Just his luck, he finally garnered up enough courage to tell her how he felt, and she was passed out.

Maybe it was a sign.

A sign to just leave well enough alone and be happy with what he had without longing for more.

Like Ashley had said earlier about him being the very best friend there ever was, that was exactly how he felt about her. The argument Savannah had used earlier about maybe getting the woman he loved was still valid, but he already had Ashley in his life, and he just couldn't risk losing her.

"Come on, sleepyhead," he whispered as he maneuvered her into his arms and stood with her, he may as well take her up to bed so she could get the rest she needed.

As he looked at her face against his shoulder he knew he had to make his peace with what was and not be greedy for more. There was no way he could live without this woman in his life, so he was going to take being best friends and be happy with it.

CHAPTER
Five

December 23rd
4:34 A.M.

He was ripped from sleep by an earth-shattering scream.

Sawyer bolted upright at the sound, and his hand went straight to the gun on the nightstand.

After the park incident yesterday, he hadn't been able to go to sleep without knowing the weapon was there if he needed it, and it looked like he was going to need it.

Bounding out of bed, he didn't bother to throw on clothes, if someone was in the house it hardly mattered that he was half-dressed, wearing only a pair of old sweatpants.

Quietly Sawyer opened his bedroom door and checked the hall.

It was empty.

The door to the bathroom was closed, as was the door to the spare bedroom. The door to Ashley's room was also closed.

Before he made a move he stood perfectly still and listened.

Nothing.

He couldn't hear footsteps, there were no thumps or bumps, and there were no more screams, but if the killer had gotten past Michael and into the house that didn't necessarily mean anything.

Had he just imagined the scream?

It wouldn't be the first time he had dreamed about Ashley being raped and murdered. In the days following her assault, he'd had almost as many nightmares as she had. While hers seemed to have faded, his hadn't. At least a couple of nights a week he jolted from sleep, dripping in sweat and ice cold, having just lost Ashley in his dreams. At least that was better than losing her in real life.

There were no more sounds and Sawyer was convinced the scream had followed him out of his nightmare. He'd give the house a quick check over, text Michael to make sure everything was okay, then he'd go back to sleep.

He was just heading toward the stairs when another scream ripped through the quiet night.

It was coming from Ashley's room.

Sawyer threw the door open, expecting to see Ashley struggling with the killer, but he didn't. Instead it was just Ashley on the bed, fighting with the covers. It looked like he wasn't the only one struggling with nightmares tonight.

Setting the gun down on the nightstand, he approached the bed carefully. Ashley was thrashing about, and he didn't want to get hit in the face, nor did he want to scare her more than she already appeared to be.

"Ash," he said, putting one knee on the bed and leaning over her, taking hold of her by the upper arms. "Ash, wake up."

She didn't hear him, still stuck in whatever terror she was dreaming about.

"Ashley," he said, louder this time, giving her a shake. "Wake up. You're dreaming. Ash, it's just a nightmare."

She whimpered. The most pitiful sound he had ever heard. He hated seeing her like this, suffering and afraid, needing him, but there was nothing he could do to help her.

"Ashley," he said again, bordering on a shout this time, "come on, wake up, now. Wake up."

He shook her harder this time, and she bolted upright, gasping, her eyes too wide, dark saucers in the dim light of the lamp. Her chest was heaving, and her gaze darted around the room before settling on him.

Seeing him didn't seem to reassure her, there was a vacant look in her eyes, mixed with terror, as though she was half awake but still half stuck in her dreams, and when she looked at him she didn't see him but whoever had haunted her nightmares.

"It's Sawyer," he spoke slowly, hoping his words could penetrate the terrified haze she was stuck in. "Ashley, it's Sawyer. You hear me? You were dreaming, you must have been having nightmares, you screamed, but you're okay, you're here in bed in my house. You're safe."

"S-Sawyer," she murmured, her eyes clearing, and her hands lifted to clutch at his shoulders.

"Right here, sweetheart." He smiled encouragingly at her, although his own heart was only just starting to slow down. Nothing scared him as much as believing that Ashley was in trouble.

"I hate nightmares," she said miserably. She was shaking and although she wasn't crying her eyes were brimming with unshed tears. She tried to move but was still tangled up in the blankets, she shoved at them, her movements panicky, but couldn't seem to untangle herself.

"Ash, calm down," he said soothingly. "Here." He gently moved her hands aside and pulled at the blankets until they loosened. He pulled one free and wrapped it around her shaking shoulders then rubbed her arms to warm her. "You want to lie down and try to go back to sleep?"

"No," she said quickly, shaking her head a little too vehemently.

"You want to get up, maybe get something to eat?" She hadn't had anything to eat yesterday since they'd gone out jogging early and then she had slept the day away.

"No, I just want to sit here for a bit. Do you mind staying?" she asked a little shyly. Obviously she hadn't heard anything he'd said to her last night about his feelings for her because if she had, she wouldn't be asking him to sit in her bed and comfort her.

"Of course not." He smiled and stretched out beside her, leaning against the headboard. Ashley immediately snuggled into him, curling into his side, her cheek on his chest, her breath warm on his skin, her hair tickling his chin. Sawyer sucked in a breath and willed his body not to respond. This wasn't about him and his desires, this was about Ashley needing comfort.

"Sorry I woke you," Ashley said, resting a hand low on his stomach.

Comfort.

This was about offering the comfort she needed, he reminded himself.

If that hand of hers dipped any lower there was a very real chance he might lose his self-control.

"Don't worry about it," he told her, stroking her hair more to give him something to do than for any other reason. "Do you want to talk about it?" Ashley didn't say anything so he wasn't sure if she did or she didn't. "Were you dreaming about him coming for you again?"

"Kind of," she whispered so softly he could barely hear her.

Taking that as a sign that she did in fact want to talk about her bad dream he continued, "You know I won't let him hurt you again. He's not going to kill you, I won't allow it."

"I know." He could feel her lips curve in a smile. "I wasn't dreaming about that. I was dreaming about that night."

She didn't have to specify which night she meant.

The night where her life had been irrevocably changed.

He thought about it every day so he could only imagine how often those events ran through Ashley's mind.

"I don't remember," she said quietly.

"Don't remember what, honey?"

"Him raping me. I remember every single second of that night except for that." She shuddered against him.

Sawyer had to hold himself very still so he didn't shudder right along with her. She never talked about this. Sometimes she would mention other bits and pieces from that night, but she had never once brought up the topic of being raped. As much as he didn't want to have this conversation with her, no one wanted to think about the woman they loved being violated like that, what Ashley felt and needed was much more important than what he wanted.

"It's probably just your brain protecting you," he said. "Blocking that out because you already have more than you can deal with."

"I feel like it shouldn't affect me," she continued. He could tell she was crying because he could feel her tears dripping down onto his bare skin. "How can it? I don't remember it."

"That's not the way it works, sweetheart," he reminded her. He knew she knew that, but he could see why she was thinking the way she was, she had so much on her plate.

"Do you think it will always affect me?"

"I don't know. I'm sure in some ways it will, but with time, and the closure of him being caught, then you'll be able to find a place where those events are a part of you, but they don't define you."

Ashley nodded but didn't say anything, and they sat there in silence for a few minutes, her crying silent tears, him just holding her and wishing he could do more.

Eventually he asked, "You want to get up? We can watch TV or play a game."

"As much as I don't want to sleep again and risk more nightmares I'm still tired, I don't know how after sleeping for almost twenty-four hours straight. Can you stay in here with me for the rest of the night?"

"Of course, I'm always here for you when you need me."

"You're the best." Ashley straightened up and kissed his cheek before snuggling back down against the mattress.

Sawyer lay down beside her and wrapped an arm around her when she settled at his side. Sleeping in the bed beside the woman he loved and not being able to do more than hold her was some kind of mixed torture because at least holding her was something, but he wanted more. So much more.

"Sweet dreams, Ash."

"Same to you," she returned sleepily.

He had no doubt that going to sleep with Ashley in his arms that his dreams would be sweeter than honey.

~

8:23 A.M.

.   .   .

Ashley woke feeling well-rested and relaxed for the first time in a long time.

Taking the sleeping pill had turned out to be a good thing. She had needed the rest, and if she hadn't taken the pill she never would have slept for so long.

The relaxed part was all Sawyer's doing though.

Falling asleep in his arms had managed to keep her nightmares at bay. And as much as she didn't really want to admit it to herself she liked this. She liked going to sleep with someone's warm body at her side, and she liked waking up to the sounds of their snoring.

Well, not anyone's snoring, but Sawyer's was definitely okay.

She smiled as she looked over at him sprawled out on the bed beside her. Ashley was glad that she felt comfortable enough around him again that she could ask him to stay in here with her when she couldn't face being alone. Now she just needed to make sure that things stayed this way. No more fantasies about kissing Sawyer. None. She couldn't risk messing things up with the best thing she had going on in her life.

Ashley was glad Sawyer had gotten some sleep. She knew he was one of those people who could get by on just a couple of hours sleep a night, but she also knew he'd been getting less than that lately because he was her bodyguard and he worried about her.

His arm was hooked around her waist, and even in sleep his grip on her was tight. What she'd said to him yesterday couldn't be truer, he was the best, best friend there ever was. She was so lucky to have him. He was the first best friend she'd ever had, in school she'd had lots of friends but no one friend who she was closer with. When she had first started working with the private security firm she hadn't ever intended to grow as close to Sawyer as she had, it had just kind of happened, and now she couldn't be more grateful. Without him she really didn't think she could have made it through these last months.

Trying her best not to wake him so he could sleep a little longer, Ashley rolled over and slid out from underneath his arm. She was just swinging her legs over the edge of the bed when she heard him stir.

"How did you sleep?"

She should have known she couldn't move without him noticing, it was like he was so attuned to her that he knew what she was going to do before she did it. "I slept well. How about you?" Ashley turned back around to face him.

"Actually, I slept great, best sleep I've had in months."

"Me too, I think it was because you were there." She smiled at him. "Thanks for last night. You know for listening to me and trying to make me feel better."

"I hope I didn't just try, I hope I *did* make you feel better."

"You did."

"Good, I'm glad. How're you feeling today?"

"Stiffer and sorer than I did yesterday, I was just going to go grab a shower, hopefully the hot water will help."

"I'll go make some breakfast while you shower," Sawyer said, climbing out of bed.

He said something else, but she didn't hear it.

Her gaze was fixed on his bare chest.

She had seen him without a top on plenty of times before, but something about this was different.

His chest was so sculpted, his six-pack the best she'd ever seen.

And she was right back to thinking about kissing him.

Not just kissing him.

Now she was thinking about doing a whole lot more.

She was thinking about the two of them naked and sweaty and in bed together, kissing, touching, making love.

"Ash?"

Somehow he had circled the bed and was standing in front of her, looking concerned.

"Are you okay? You looked like you spaced out. Is it your head? Are you feeling dizzy? Nauseous? Should I call Brian?"

Ashley forced herself to focus and stop thinking these ridiculous thoughts. "I'm fine, just lost in thought." She was sure her cheeks had turned bright red, and she was worried that what she'd been thinking was written all over her face, but there wasn't anything she could do about that.

"Okay," he agreed, not looking altogether convinced. "Are you okay to walk on your ankle?"

Pleased to have something to distract her, Ashley looked down at her ankle, it was black and blue and swollen to twice its usual size but it didn't hurt too badly. "It's okay," she said, rotating it.

"We'll strap it when you finish up in the shower. Call out if you need anything."

"I will," she murmured distractedly as she watched Sawyer walk out of the room. Why did he have to sleep half-naked? And why did he have to look so good in a pair of old sweats? And why did those sweatpants have to hang so low on his hips very nearly revealing something that would ruin her self control?

Rousing herself, Ashley grabbed some clothes and limped off to the bathroom.

She paused at the mirror and studied her reflection. The twenty-four hours worth of sleep she'd gotten had erased some of the dark circles under her eyes, and her color was better, but...

Ashley traced her fingertips along the angry red scars.

People kept telling her that they would fade in time, but it was hard to believe it right now. And even if they did fade they were never going to disappear. She had to find a way to live with them like she had to find a way to live with everything else.

Last night she'd confessed something to Sawyer she hadn't even verbalized to herself yet. She knew she had been raped, she knew it but it didn't feel real because she didn't remember it, which made her feel like she didn't have a right to be affected by it.

It was odd, she hadn't thought a lot about what had happened to her, and her nightmares had faded after the first week or so, but now after learning that the end was in sight, she had her first nightmare in months, and her feelings about the assault were shoving their way past the barriers she had erected and into her mind. It was like the protective little bubble she had been in, focusing only on the man being caught, was slowly going down and all those other thoughts and feelings were creeping in.

She shoved aside those thoughts, it was Christmas and she was just going to enjoy the next few days, she had the rest of her life to learn to deal with everything else.

Her ankle was sore so she didn't stay long in the shower, just gave her long hair a quick shampoo and condition, then gently scrubbed herself, careful not to split open any of the scratches on her arms and face. When she was done she dried off, threw on sweats, left her hair to air dry, and headed downstairs to find Sawyer in the kitchen.

"Savannah brought cinnamon rolls," he called over his shoulder as he pulled out a bag of flour.

"What are you doing?" she asked, looking at the kitchen counters, they looked like a supermarket had exploded in here, there were bags and jars everywhere.

"We're baking," Sawyer turned around and grinned at her.

"*We're* baking?" she echoed. "You remember who you're talking to right? The woman who can't even boil water, who burns everything she touches, who is yet to cook a single meal even though she is twenty-four years old."

Sawyer laughed. "It'll be fine, we're only making gingerbread men. I wanted to do a gingerbread house, but I thought it was a bit above your skill level," he snickered.

She glowered at him. "Isn't your sister going to be baking her annual gingerbread masterpiece tomorrow anyway? If you want gingerbread just have some of hers."

"Come on, it'll be fun," Sawyer wheedled. "And Christmassy. The recipe is easy, and when we're done we get to ice them and decorate them."

"Okay, it does kind of sound like fun, but I hold no responsibility if they end up tasting like garbage."

"Great." Sawyer beamed excitedly. "Grab the butter, we need half a cup, and we have to throw it in the mixer with two-thirds of a cup of super fine sugar and one-third of a cup of honey."

"Maybe you should do the measuring so I don't mess up," she said, hobbling over to the chair Sawyer had set up at the counter.

"You'll do fine," he said.

As carefully as she could she measured out the ingredients and poured them into the mixer. "Now what?"

"Now you have to cream them."

"I have to add cream?"

Sawyer laughed again. "No we have to cream the ingredients together, it means mix them until they're kind of soft and fluffy."

"Then why don't they just say that?" She didn't get cooking, it all looked so simple when other people did it, but when she tried it turned into a disaster. And baking was even worse, half the time she didn't even know what they were trying to say.

"Turn it on," Sawyer told her.

She flipped the switch, and the machine whooshed to life spitting chunks of butter and puffs of sugar everywhere.

"Turn it off," Sawyer shouted, laughing so hard he could barely get the words out. "You have to put the lid on so it doesn't do that."

"Then why didn't you tell me? You know I'm terrible at this." She pouted.

"Here you go, try again." He handed her the lid to the mixer, and she put it on then cautiously turned the machine back on. Again it whirred to life, but this time the contents of the bowl stayed inside the bowl.

"I did it." She beamed, proud of herself.

"Told you, you could."

"How will I know when it's creamed?"

"You'll know," Sawyer said confidently.

"Yeah, right," she said, with much less confidence. She watched the swirling ingredients like a hawk, and a minute or so later they started to turn into a soft, fluffy looking concoction, just like Sawyer had said they would. "Are they done?"

"They are, see you could tell."

"Only because you explained it to me." She switched off the mixer then looked at Sawyer expectantly. "What next?"

"Crack an egg in there and mix it through until you can't see any egg."

With a small flicker of confidence, Ashley cracked the egg, turned the mixer back on, and then off again when the egg looked like it was all mixed in. "What do I do now?"

"You need to add two cups of flour and the ginger and mixed spice, and mix it in with the wooden spoon."

Ashley did as Sawyer instructed and was pleased when the mixture started to form a dough. "I'm doing it," she squealed excitedly.

"You sure are. Now take it out and put it on the counter and knead in the rest of the flour so that the dough is smooth."

She added the last of the flour and kneaded the dough, enjoying the feel of the mixture on her fingers. It was very therapeutic, she could see why Savannah loved to bake. "All done. Do we cut out the shapes and bake it now?"

"It has to sit in the fridge for thirty minutes first."

"Okay," she said, taking the cling wrap Sawyer passed her and wrapping up the dough.

"You're enjoying this," he said.

"Maybe," she acknowledged with a giggle.

"You have butter on your face," Sawyer told her, brushing a thumb across her cheek and wiping it away.

At his touch she felt a kind of warm, fluttery feeling in her stomach.

She felt something for Sawyer.

Something that went beyond just friendship.

She'd never felt it before, but they'd never spent time like this together in the past.

Now she knew that wanting to kiss Sawyer had nothing to do with just being grateful to have him in her life, it was because she cared about him. She might even love him.

"Want to play something while we wait? Poker? Or Go Fish?" Sawyer teased because she was notoriously bad at card games, almost as bad as she was at cooking, and Go Fish and Snap were about all she could manage.

"Yeah, sure," she agreed, disconcerted by her realization that she might very well be in love with her best friend.

"Great, let's strap your ankle, eat some of Savannah's cinnamon rolls, and then play Go Fish, or maybe since you aced the cooking you're ready to try a big girl game."

Unable to come up with a witty comeback she just smiled at him, maybe a little goofily.

She was in major trouble now.

If she was falling for her best friend at the very time when she needed a best friend more than anything else then maybe it was time to move out of Sawyer's house.

As much as she'd miss seeing him every day she couldn't risk losing him.

~

11:52 A.M.

Morgan Hawksworth dashed across the street from her favorite café back to the FBI building.

From the temperature, she was surprised it wasn't pouring snow out here, but as it had been every day for the last month the sky was clear and a pale watery blue, the sun was shining, but it was as cold as though she were living inside an ice block.

She hated the cold, and not just because it was cold, but because she knew the power that it possessed and how dangerous it could be. She didn't think that even if she lived to be a hundred she would ever learn to be comfortable with the cold again. Some things you just couldn't take back and what she had lived through was one of those things.

With two sandwiches and two cups of coffee in her hands, she ducked back through the door and immediately felt the warmth envelop her like an old friend. She breathed a sigh of relief and headed for the stairs. She hated small enclosed spaces almost as much as she hated the cold, and avoided lifts wherever she could.

For her the cold wasn't just some nuisance, she didn't care about having to shovel driveways, or frozen pipes, or slippery patches of ice. The cold scared her. Terrified her. Having to be out in it still almost gave her panic attacks despite the fact that many years had passed since her ordeal.

That was one of the things she liked about her job. She could focus on other people and their ordeals without having to dwell on her own. Not that she wanted other people to suffer. If it was possible she would eliminate all crime, but since that wasn't possible the best she could do was help them through it and try to give them closure by finding the people who had hurt them, and making sure they were held accountable for their actions.

It was a good job, and she was grateful for it every day.

"Here you go," she said, reaching hers and Jett's desks and setting his coffee and sandwich down. "Next time you get lunch."

"I had to call Savannah," Jett said.

"I know, I know." She rolled her eyes as she began the process of removing her layers of clothing that were supposed to help keep the cold away from her skin but more often than not failed. She couldn't really be angry with her partner though, he and his wife had just found out they were expecting their first baby, who wouldn't be excited about that? "How's she doing?"

"Great, she's still got morning sickness, but we are both just so thrilled. She's only six weeks along so it's going to be hard to wait out the next seven and a half months." Jett was positively beaming this morning, his blue eyes were sparkling, and despite the grim nature of the cases they were working he hadn't been able to wipe a smile off his face.

Morgan set her gloves, her two scarves—one she wrapped around her neck and tucked under her coat the other she wound around her chin and mouth, her beanie, her coat, and her extra sweater down on one side of her desk. Then she looked up to see Jett watching her, looking all FBI like. "What?"

"You going to tell me why you hate the cold?"

"Because it's cold, that's no secret," she said vaguely.

"You don't just not like the cold, you *hate* it. In my experience, people only hate things they have reason to hate. It's a strong emotion and usually comes from somewhere."

Why did she have to get assigned a partner who was so intuitive?

She didn't want to talk about her past, she didn't want to have to explain what she'd been through, she didn't want to have to see the doubt in Jett's eyes as he wondered how he could possibly trust her to have his back once he knew the truth about her.

Instead of thinking up a lie, Morgan just shrugged. "Let's just leave it at I hate the cold, and I'm always going to hate the cold."

"For now." Jett nodded.

"No, not *for now*," she said, bristling. Who did Jett think he was? If she said she didn't want to talk about it he should respect that.

Although she got the feeling that Jett did what he thought was best regardless of what others thought about it. "Consider it a closed topic."

"We're partners, I know we haven't known each other that long, but you'll tell me when you trust me."

He said it so confidently that she almost screamed.

She knew he was wrong, she wasn't ever going to talk about her past, not with anyone, but that he didn't know he was wrong was extremely irritating.

Jett chuckled. "I'm annoying you."

That he didn't sound like he cared only further frustrated her. He was the most arrogant guy she had ever met. As much as she wanted to growl at him, instead she schooled her features into a mask of calm and slid into her chair, taking her time unwrapping her sandwich and then taking a long drink of her coffee, enjoying the way the burning liquid scalded her throat all the way down.

"I'm not annoyed," she said when she was sure it would come out borderline disinterested instead of red hot with aggravation.

"Oh, you're annoyed." Jett was leaning back in his chair watching her with amusement. "You want to throw that coffee at me, don't you?"

"No," she muttered, "but only because I don't want to waste the coffee."

Jett laughed loudly, then he sobered. "I'm not trying to bother you, Morgan, I just want you to know I'm here for you, if you ever want to talk I'm here."

Although she had no intention of ever talking with her partner about her past she appreciated that he wanted to be there for her. "Thanks, Jett." Before she could say more, Jett's computer beeped, and when he glanced over at it a huge grin broke out on his face. "What?"

"We got a hit."

"A hit? On the DNA from the serial rapist and murderer?" Morgan had been hoping that they would but had also been trying not to get her hopes up too high because she had learned early on in her career that there were no guarantees in this job. Sometimes you worked a case as hard as you could, looking into every avenue that presented itself and still you couldn't solve it.

"Yep." Jett was grinning even more than he'd been when he told her the news of Savannah's pregnancy.

"What's his name?"

"Evander Hurley."

Evander Hurley, it sounded like such an innocuous name, like he could be anyone, your dentist, your kid's teacher, the man who owned the local mom and pop store. Morgan always thought that evil people should have evil names so that everyone knew to stay far away from them.

"What's he in the system for?" she asked.

Jett scanned his computer screen, reading the details then said, "Looks like stalking. Several complaints from the same woman that he kept turning up at her job, her home, her gym, her hairdresser, everywhere she went he went. He was relentless. He'd scream obscenities at her and threaten that one day he'd get to her."

"Did he?" Was this woman Evander's first victim?

"No, doesn't look like it."

"If he hated her so much did he ever make a move and try to kill her?" It seemed logical if this man hated her that at some point he would have tried something.

"Looks like the woman was married to a cop who managed to scare the guy enough to keep him away."

"Do we have an address for Evander?"

"The stalking charges were from three years ago, we can check this out, but chances are he moved."

"Three years ago, so right before the murders started. We should talk to this woman."

"We can't," Jett said.

"Why?"

"She passed away just a month before the murders started. Cancer. It looks like that was why the cases never went anywhere. Evander Hurley was arrested a couple of times for trespassing, there was a restraining order in place, but then the woman died, and the case died along with her."

"All of the victims looked the same, and we theorized that even though he changed up his method of strangling them since he didn't change victimology it was because what they looked like was important. If he was fixated on this woman and she died before he could get to her, he could be killing these women as surrogates. Is there a picture of the woman?"

"Petunia Smith was twenty-three years old when she died, she had dark brown eyes and long dark hair."

"So she matches these victims. We need to see if Evander Hurley is still at the address on file, and if he's not, we need to find where he is now." Morgan was feeling energized. They had their guy now they just had to find him.

~

1:41 P.M.

It felt good to be vindicated.

Evander had changed a lot from the quiet, shy boy he had been when Petunia Smith had decided it would be fun to ruin his life.

He was never going to be that kid again.

Gone were the long gangly limbs, in their place was a toned, muscled physique, gone were the thick glasses, in their place were contact lenses. Gone was the acne, his skin now smooth and tanned, and gone was the timid demeanor that invited people to take advantage, in its place was a confidence he could never have envisioned he would one day possess.

It had taken him years to get to this place, ten years to be exact. In January it would be ten years to the day when Petunia's games had spun so far out of control there had almost been no going back.

He had been sixteen then, now he was twenty-six, a successful motivational speaker who spoke on the values of rebuilding your life to become stronger, smarter, better than you'd been before. Little did anyone know that when he spoke about seeking help, talking about things, finding your own inner peace, deciding who you wanted to be and then plotting a course to get there, that his methods of improving himself had also included revenge.

It was revenge that had saved his life, not therapy and rebuilding himself. But it probably wasn't appropriate to preach to others that they should track down the person who had destroyed them and punish them until they knew what it was like to feel afraid of being alive, to hate yourself so much you wanted to rip yourself apart inch by inch until you became the nothing you felt like.

Petunia Smith.

Pretty, popular, a cheerleader, the girl in his class that all the boys wanted to bed and all the girls wanted to be.

Unfortunately who she was on the inside didn't match her looks on the outside.

There wasn't a single attractive thing about Petunia aside from her face. She was a cruel, ugly, deceitful person who had used her looks to entice him, leading him straight into a trap, then hurting him worse than he'd known it was possible to be hurt.

Because of her, he had tried to end his life.

Because of her, he had grown to hate himself.

Because of her, he had grown to hate the whole world.

Then because of her, he had grown strong.

It was just a shame that she had died before he'd had a chance to wrap his hands around her neck and squeeze the life out of her. Still, she was dead, and that was a good thing. Even the universe knew what a despicable person she was and struck her down with a fatal disease.

But with her dead that feeling of being lost started to creep back in.

He had felt adrift in the ocean of life with no purpose. After graduating high school his whole focus had been growing strong and punishing Petunia for what she had done. He had tracked her down, determined to make her feel the fear that he had felt, knowing he was coming for her. If it weren't for that stupid cop husband, then he wouldn't have been robbed of his chance to get vengeance.

At loose ends, he had found another way to feed that beast inside him.

A beast that had been created that fateful day ten years ago.

If it wasn't for Petunia there would be no beast. She was its mother, and she was responsible for everything it had lured him to do. Before that day he had never laid a hand on another human being, never even thought of doing it, but now taking lives had become his life, his purpose.

It was the only way he could get the revenge Petunia's death had robbed him of. So he found beautiful young women who looked just like her and did to them what he wished he could have done to Petunia. Then he thanked them for being the stand-ins he had needed and walked away, ready to live his life until the cravings became too strong and he needed to kill again.

Although a beast lived inside him, he wasn't a monster.

He was a victim.

Just a victim looking to rebuild his life and grow strong.

And with every life he took he did grow stronger.

Now he felt invincible.

Their lives so he could live.

Which was why it was so imperative that he find Ashley Fallon.

It wasn't about self-preservation, he was too smart, too strong, the FBI would never find him. It was about finishing what he started. Petunia had slipped through his fingers but Ashley wouldn't.

The universe was on his side again, validating that he bore no responsibility for who he had become. That lay firmly on the shoulders of Petunia and those who had helped her play out her sick game.

Early yesterday morning he had been wandering through one of the parks near his house when he had seen her.

Ashley Fallon and a man out jogging.

He had been right all along, she wasn't dead, merely hiding and hoping that he would lose interest and go away.

Only he hadn't lost interest in her, and he wasn't going anywhere until he knew she was dead.

When he'd seen her for a moment he had been sure his eyes must be playing tricks on him. It was dark, and although the park had solar power lights along the walking tracks, it was still gloomy and hard to see clearly.

But when he'd sneaked closer he saw he'd been right.

It really was her.

As much as he'd wanted to just run up and grab her, he'd seen the bulge at the man's waist. He was armed, and Evander hadn't been. So he had intended to hang back, follow them, and find out where she was hiding out. Then he could make his move.

However, the universe had other ideas.

It had offered her up on a silver platter.

She had fallen down the hill and landed just a couple of yards away from where he was hiding in the trees. Ashley had been dazed and confused, and he had thought that getting her would be easy, but she had seen him and started running, straight into the arms of her armed friend, who had quickly pulled out a weapon.

Knowing when he was beaten, Evander had quickly fled.

He hadn't gone far though. Just back to his car to hide out until it was safe to start his search.

Now he was walking the streets trying to find her. He knew she had to be around here somewhere because you didn't travel too far to go jogging at five in the morning. The house where she was living was around here someplace.

Once the dark returned, he would get out his flying drone and see if he could use it to get a glimpse inside as many of the houses in the area as he could to see if he could locate her.

He would do it.

It might take him days, or weeks, or possibly even months, but he had all the time in the world and he *would* find and kill Ashley Fallon, and anyone who tried to stop him.

Evander felt no desire to kill anyone else, he had no grudge against them and they served no purpose in satiating the beast, but he had to kill Ashley. He *had* to. It was like a compulsion, he must finish what he'd started. He couldn't let any of them live, he had to claim her life. It was like if he didn't then the beast would turn on him and consume him instead of him consuming others.

He turned the corner into the next street, he knew the chances of him randomly finding which of the hundreds of houses was the one Ashley was in was slim. Perhaps if the drone idea didn't work he would try to find out who the man was. It was obvious that she was staying in his house, so if he could get a name then he'd be able to get an address, and then he'd get Ashley.

It was for the best for her as well that he ended her life.

She had to live with what he had done to her, and he knew what it was like to have to live after being hurt so deeply it left festering sores that no one could see that you were lucky if they ever healed and became scars.

Evander couldn't do that to another human being.

Not after living through it himself.

He killed the women in place of Petunia, whose life he wasn't able to take, but he also did it for them.

So that they didn't have to live with being raped.

Ending Ashley's life was as much for her benefit as it was for his own.

~

6:20 P.M.

"Are you sure you don't want to come in?"

Ashley looked up to see Sawyer standing in the door. "I'm good out here," she replied. She was sitting in the backyard enjoying the cold night air.

"Are you sitting in a tree?" Sawyer asked, amused, as he walked toward her.

"I like sitting in trees," she replied. She'd always had a fascination with climbing trees, ever since she was a very little girl. Several summers, she and her dad had spent weeks planning and building tree houses in their yard. Those were good times, fun times, out in the sun, sawing and hammering planks of wood, her mom would bring them out glasses of fresh, homemade lemonade and homemade chocolate chip cookies.

"Oh, I remember." Sawyer stood underneath the tree, looking up at her. "I also remember the great tree climbing races of the summer before last."

She remembered that too. It had been lots of fun. She and her friends from work had had a Fourth of July party, and the boys had been being boys, thinking they were all tough and strong, and she'd told them she could make it to the top of a tree before they could. Being the competitive bunch they were, they'd all agreed. "I won that race."

"Yeah, but you fell out of the tree and broke your arm, gave yourself a concussion, and cracked two ribs," Sawyer reminded her. "We spent the rest of the day in the ER."

"But I won."

"You did." Sawyer laughed. "I'm going to cook dinner. Sure you don't want to come in and help?"

"I think we've tempted fate enough today."

"The gingerbread came out great, and admit it, you had fun."

"Okay, okay," she agreed. "I had fun baking the gingerbread Santas and Mrs. Clauses." They'd made a dozen couples, and it had been fun decorating them, Sawyer had even shown her how to pipe the icing on then use a small knife to smooth it out so that they could add different colors to different parts of the cookies. "But I'm just enjoying the peace and quiet out here right now. I'll come inside in a bit, okay?"

"All right. Call if you need anything, and be careful climbing back down with that bad ankle, you don't want another fall after yesterday's."

"I'll be careful," she promised.

When Sawyer had gone back inside she leaned back against the tree trunk and looked up at the stars. She would love to visit somewhere in the middle of nowhere one day just so she could lie on the ground at night and look up at the black sky to see millions of twinkling diamonds looking down at her. Ashley bet it would be amazing, nothing like looking at the stars in the city when all the light from the houses, and shops, and streetlights made it so you didn't get the full effect.

As much fun as she and Sawyer had had baking the gingerbread and playing Go Fish—he beat her in every game they had played—she kept thinking about that night in September.

Try as she did to banish her thoughts it was getting harder and harder to do.

Sawyer was good at keeping her distracted but what was she going to do when after Christmas she spoke with Brady, Ryan, or Paige about moving out of Sawyer's house and staying with a different bodyguard until this guy was caught?

Evander Hurley.

That was his name.

Jett and Morgan had stopped by after lunch to tell her they got a DNA match and to ask her to look at a picture and see if she could identify him as the man who had attacked her.

She hadn't wanted to.

That face already haunted her, and she didn't want to ever see it again.

But she made herself do it, and it was him.

Evander Hurley was the man who had raped and strangled her with a metal chain and then tracked her down in the hospital to try to finish her off.

According to Jett and Morgan, although they had his name they couldn't find an address. The only one they had been able to find was an out of state one and it looked like he hadn't been there in months. Evander worked as a motivational speaker but had nothing booked for the coming weeks, and hadn't done any talks ever since the attack on her.

Because he had something other than work to occupy his time.

Her.

He wasn't working because he was no doubt trying to figure out if she was still alive and where she was hiding out.

This was almost worse than when they hadn't known who he was.

Ashley had thought that once they had a name it would be so easy. They would just go and arrest him, and she would move on with her life.

But that wasn't how it was playing out.

The FBI had his DNA and his name, they knew everything about him except the only thing that mattered.

Where he was.

For the first time she felt confused about the whole situation. She wanted Evander caught so she didn't have to live with the fear of him coming after her. And yet at the same time that meant that she would be leaving Sawyer's house and she wouldn't get to see him every day. And as the fear of Evander coming after her again started to fade—she knew that Jett and Morgan would find him—the fear of having to finally face what had happened to her and find a way to live with it was growing.

What a mess.

She was a mess.

Her life was a mess.

This whole thing was one big gigantic mess, and the one person who usually made her feel grounded when the world was tossing and twirling around her was now the one person she was afraid to get any closer to.

Sawyer was going to be so angry and hurt when he found out she was leaving. He would think it was because she didn't trust him to keep her safe, or because he had done something to upset her, and she couldn't tell him it was because she was falling for him.

Something caught her gaze.

A blinking light?

No, it looked like light reflecting off something, like a piece of glass or metal, but it was up too high, and it was moving, she couldn't figure out what it was.

Ashley wasn't sure what it was, but she had a bad feeling about it. Her instincts were saying something was wrong, and she wasn't going to argue with them.

As quickly as she could she started climbing down. She was only about ten feet up but between her ankle and her bruised and battered body it was taking longer than she liked.

Something went crash nearby like it had been knocked over.

A cat meowed loudly, and then a dog barked.

Was it just a clash between cat and dog or had something startled them both?

"Sawyer," she yelled as loudly as she could. If someone was out there, then she wanted Sawyer here. Now.

In less than five seconds she heard the back door swing open and footsteps coming toward her. "Ash? You okay?"

"I heard something," she told him when he reached her.

He reached up and wrapped his hands around her waist, lifting her the rest of the way down to the ground. "Heard what?"

"I don't know. I saw something reflecting light, and I started climbing down, then I heard a crash. What if he's out there?" They knew who Evander was, and they knew he was resourceful, he'd tracked her down at the hospital after all, so it was plausible he had learned Sawyer's identity and tracked her down here.

Sawyer muttered a curse under his breath. "I left my gun inside, I thought you just got stuck in the tree. Get inside, lock the doors, get my gun, and hide," he rattled off orders.

"No." She shook her head firmly, she wasn't going anywhere on her own. "I'm safer with you."

He looked like he was going to argue but instead shoved her behind him. "We'll check the yard then call the cops, have them come and check things out properly. I'm not taking any chances, not after we know someone was at the park yesterday when you fell."

Sticking close to Sawyer, she followed him as he cautiously made his way around the small fenced in yard. They were just moving to check behind the shed when she saw something round appearing over the top of it.

"Sawyer, look," she squawked in a panicked whisper.

He took one look then threw them both around the other side of the shed, shoving her up against the fence and covering her body with his own. "Don't move," he whispered in her ear."

Her fingers curled into his sweater and held on tight as he carefully moved his head to look around the shed while making sure his body still covered hers.

Then he laughed.

"What is it?" she asked, confused.

"Come see." He gently uncurled her fingers and took her hand, pulling her out into the open and pointing at something floating up toward the sky.

A balloon.

With a small plastic box tied to its string.

In the box was a family of dolls.

"Is that what you saw?" Sawyer asked.

"Probably," she said, allowing a small smile to help calm her racing heart.

"It probably belongs to the Wilkins kids from behind us," Sawyer said, releasing her hand to climb up onto the shed roof so he could grab hold of the string. "We'll take it back to them in the morning."

If she hadn't panicked and had just taken a moment to look properly at what had caught her attention, she would have seen that it was just an innocent balloon. The sight of it had probably startled the cat and dog, and one of them had knocked something over.

"Don't worry, Ash." Sawyer jumped down beside her and took her hand again. "We're both on edge right now, it's perfectly normal. It was just a balloon, no one is out here."

"You're right," she agreed, squeezing his hand, it was going to be hard to say goodbye to him, she had to make the most of the next couple of days because once she moved out things would never be the same between them again.

~

7:04 P.M.

Sawyer was glad that Jett and Morgan were making progress in finding the killer because the stress was really starting to get to both him and Ashley.

When he'd seen that balloon rising over the shed for one horrifying second he'd thought it was Evander Hurley. He'd thrown himself and Ashley out of the way, using his body as a shield to protect her, and cursed his stupidity for coming outside unarmed. When Ashley had screamed his name he'd thought at best she was just stuck in the tree unable to climb down with her bad ankle, or at worst she'd fallen out of the tree and injured herself. If he had known that she'd screamed for help, he would have grabbed his gun before heading into the yard.

Seeing that balloon was such a relief.

Now that it was over and he knew Ashley was safe it was kind of funny.

He could tell she was still tense. Luckily he had the perfect way for her to relax.

"I have a surprise for you inside," he told Ashley. She'd been so jittery lately that he wanted to do something special to try to take her mind off everything that had been going on.

"You spoil me." Ashley squeezed his hand. "You don't have to do nice things for me, I'll be okay."

"Course you will. No one's tougher than you. I wanted to do this for you, if I could I would have taken you out but since I can't..." he opened the back door, and Ashley gasped when she saw what was inside.

"Oh, Sawyer," she gushed, letting go of his hand, she rushed over to the table. "Candles, and the good china, it's like we're at a fancy restaurant only better because you did this especially for me."

"Only the best for my girl. Dinner's almost ready, why don't you go upstairs get all dressed up and I'm going to go put on my best suit. We're having a night out, only we're having it in."

"You're the best." Ashley beamed, all traces of anxiety gone from her face, now her eyes were sparkling with excitement, and her cheeks were tinted with pink. "I'll be right back."

While Ashley hurried up the stairs as quickly as she could with her ankle, Sawyer checked on the dinner, Ashley's favorites, and then also headed upstairs to change. He put on his best suit, a pale blue shirt, and a brighter blue tie that he knew matched his eyes. He ran a brush through his hair and then stopped and looked at himself in the mirror.

He looked nervous.

Since his last attempt to tell Ashley how he felt about her had failed he would try again tonight. He had the special candlelight dinner, and he had a little gift for her.

Sawyer pulled the small jewelry box out of the top dresser drawer. He stared at it for a moment then opened it up, inside nestled a set of pearl earrings and a matching pearl necklace. They used to belong to his mother, but after she passed away, he and Savannah had divided up the jewelry so they each had some to remember their mother by.

While this wasn't an engagement ring it certainly said how serious he was about Ashley. Since their father had died when he and Savannah were still young they had basically been raised by their mother, and both of them had been close with her right up until her death a couple of years ago. There was only one person he would give this to, and she was currently changing in the room across the hall.

Slipping the box into his pocket, he headed back to the kitchen to check on dinner. Everything was cooking nicely, although he would have preferred Ashley hadn't been sitting outside alone in the backyard in the dark, it had given him time to cook dinner without her hovering. Since she wasn't a very good cook, today's gingerbread aside, she usually sat in the kitchen and chatted with him while he was preparing meals.

"H-hmm."

He turned around and his jaw literally dropped.

Ashley was standing at the bottom of the stairs dressed in a slinky black dress with a plunging neckline very nearly revealing her firm, round breasts, and clung to her slender frame. The black of the dress complimented her pale skin and dark hair, making her look like a sexy Snow White. She'd curled her long hair so it hung in soft waves around her shoulders, and she'd added just the right amount of makeup, her lips the sexiest shade of red.

She looked like a goddess.

"Speechless, huh? Should I take that as a compliment?" Ashley grinned at him.

"Oh, yeah." He drew in a shaky breath. This was supposed to be about cheering Ashley up not him lusting over her. Rousing himself out of this lust-filled haze, he walked over and took her elbow. "I'll show you to your seat." She walked a little awkwardly, and he glanced down to see she was wearing heels. "Ash, you have a bad ankle, you should have gone with flats."

"They don't go with this outfit," she replied. He couldn't argue with that, he loved her in heels.

After he pushed in her chair, he went to get the first course. "Appetizers," he said, setting her plate down in front of her.

"Stuffed mushrooms," she squealed. "Your stuffed mushrooms are my favorite."

"I know." He smiled, pleased she was so happy. He loved seeing her like this, all relaxed and carefree.

"I can't believe you did all of this while I was sitting outside, you are amazing. I don't say that often enough."

Subconsciously his free hand touched the box in his pocket. If he was going to give it to her and tell her that he liked her, he should do it now and not ruin the whole meal by being too nervous to enjoy it.

"I mean it, Sawyer," Ashley continued, "I can't imagine not having you in my life. The only reason I've made it through these last few months is because of you. You've given me everything I needed. I love you so much, you're the best friend I could have ever had, and I hope that we're going to be friends for the rest of our lives, I don't want anything to ever come between us."

His eyebrows scrunched together. "What would come between us?" Did she know that he liked her? Was this her way of letting him down gently?

"I don't know, I just worry about losing you. You're the closest thing I have to family, and I love you so much."

Just not in the same way he loved her.

Did he need to be hit over the head with it?

She didn't love him.

All she felt for him was friendship.

And she didn't want him to do anything to ruin that.

If that wasn't a clear enough answer then he didn't know what would be.

It was time to let go of any notion that he and Ashley could one day be more than friends.

Time to *really* let it go.

Time to be content with what he had without seeking more.

Removing any disappointment and heartbreak from his face and voice, he smiled at her. "I love you too, Ash, and nothing is ever going to change that. You and I will still be causing havoc together when we're in a nursing home."

She giggled and relaxed. "What's for main course?"

"Guess," he said, relaxing himself. Ashley as a friend was still a pretty amazing thing to have, he was a lucky guy just to have her in his life.

"Fettuccine Alfredo?"

"Bingo."

"And dessert?"

"You tell me?"

"Chocolate mousse?"

"You got it."

"These stuffed mushrooms are to die for. If you ever get tired of being a bodyguard I think you can make a career as a chef."

"My dad was a chef before Savannah and I were born," he told Ashley.

"I didn't know that. Is that why you love to cook and Savannah loves to bake?"

"Probably. He changed jobs once he had us so he could make more money and be home with us in the evenings, but he always loved to cook. Those are some of my happiest memories of my childhood, in the kitchen, all of us together, cooking a special meal." He smiled at the memories.

"It's nice you have those memories of him. It's hard not having your parents around anymore. When you're a kid you think they're going to live forever," Ashley said wistfully.

Not wanting to give her time to dwell on sad things and let her mood slip, he asked, "You ready for the fettuccine?"

"Let's dance," Ashley announced.

"Dance?"

"Let's put on Christmas carols and just dance."

"On your ankle?" he asked, the prospect of holding Ashley up close against his body, wearing that dress, was not going to help his keep things platonic vow.

"Please." She gave him that puppy dog look he could never say no to.

"Okay," he relented, switching on the hi-fi.

As Christmas music filled the house, Ashley stood and took his hand and wrapped her other arm around his waist, settling herself against his chest and resting her head on his shoulder. She felt so good in his arms. All warm and soft and feminine. She had no idea how crazy she drove him.

They slow danced to Bing Crosby's White Christmas and it took every ounce of his self-restraint not to throw her down on the floor and make love to her in front of the Christmas tree.

"This is nice," she murmured.

He couldn't deny that.

Once again the woman he loved was in his arms, and once again it wasn't in the way he wanted. It seemed he was a glutton for punishment.

~

11:35 P.M.

Christmas Eve.

In less than thirty minutes it was going to be Christmas Eve.

Aurora Crowley had mixed feelings about the coming days.

Two years ago her life had been thrown into chaos when her brother had gotten himself mixed up in something dangerous, getting himself murdered. When she'd gone to stay at his house for a few weeks to pack up his things she had very nearly been murdered herself.

The fear she had felt in those few hours had faded, but it hadn't gone.

It still lurked there, at the back of her mind, a part of her daily life. She didn't like to talk about it because she didn't want Brady to worry about her.

And that was the reason she had mixed feelings about that Christmas Eve two years ago. As terrifying as it had been it was also the day she met Brady. At first she hadn't known whether she could trust him or not, but her instincts had said she could, and now they were happily married.

She loved Brady so much. He had retired from the police force shortly after they'd met and had partnered in a private security firm with an old friend of his, another retired cop Skylar Wyatt. A year ago, Wyatt had lost his wife and had decided he had to move on with his life, and now Brady ran the firm with two other retired cops Paige Hood and Ryan Xander.

They had gotten married just two months after meeting and had both sold their respective apartments to buy this house together. Aurora loved their home, and she had gone all out decorating it for Christmas.

There wasn't a single room that wasn't strung up with garlands and lights and dozens of Christmas decorations.

Part of the point of spending so much time decorating was to try to keep out those bad memories.

It hadn't worked.

They were still there.

Jabbing at her brain, refusing to be ignored.

Aurora took her rag doll and sat on the floor in front of the tree. The ragdoll looked exactly like one she'd had as a child but lost in one of the many moves her family had made when she was a kid. Her brother had bought it for her as kind of a peace offering to help mend the gap that had grown between them because of the bad choices he insisted on making. He had never gotten a chance to give it to her because he'd been murdered, but somehow the doll had survived the trashing of her brother's house, and she was so glad it had.

Her head darted up when she heard something go thump somewhere in the quiet house.

She began to shake.

That was exactly how that Christmas Eve had started.

Was someone other than herself and Brady in here?

What should she do?

Should she go and find what made the sound? Should she find somewhere and hide? Should she arm herself with a weapon?

Her ears strained, waiting to hear something else, footsteps, breaking glass, sounds of a fight between Brady and the intruder.

But she heard nothing.

The house was completely silent.

"You're being silly," Aurora whispered aloud. "There is no one there. It's just your mind playing tricks on you. You're perfectly safe here. Brady is asleep upstairs, he won't let anyone hurt you. This isn't two years ago."

She was just starting to calm down when someone suddenly loomed over her.

Aurora screamed.

The person reached down and picked her up.

It wasn't until she was cradled in a pair of arms that she realized it was only her husband.

"I called your name, but you were too busy talking to yourself," Brady said as he sat them both down on the sofa.

"I didn't hear you," she said, struggling to calm her ragged breaths.

"I can see that," Brady said. "What were you doing down here?"

"Just looking at the tree," she said vaguely, Brady would be annoyed with her if he learned she'd been hiding the fact that she still struggled to cope with what had happened and hadn't said anything to him.

"Lying, babe? You know I hate that." Her husband was one of those blunt people who didn't play games, he just told it like it was, he was never cruel about it though, and he usually tempered his honesty with charm, although it seemed like tonight he wasn't going to do that.

"I *was* looking at the tree," Aurora countered defensively. She'd just been thinking painful thoughts and reliving painful memories while doing it.

"You didn't nearly have a heart attack when I walked over because you were looking at the Christmas tree and thinking about what a great holiday we're going to have. You were thinking about what happened Christmas Eve two years ago." Brady had her on his lap, his arms locked around her, his dark eyes watching her carefully ready to pounce on any lie she told.

"I was," she admitted, it was probably best to stick with telling the truth wherever possible.

"I hate that you were hurt," her husband's eyes clouded over, filled with pain and regret, and he brushed the back of his knuckles across her cheek.

"It wasn't your fault," she reminded him.

"It kind of was."

"It wasn't," she said fiercely. "You saved my life that night and blew your cover in the process. We both almost died because you didn't want to let those men hurt me." Aurora shuddered as she said the words and Brady tightened his hold on her.

"Do you still think about it a lot? And don't lie to me, darlin'," he warned.

Aurora hesitated. She didn't want to lie to her husband, but she didn't want to worry him either. She had dealt with what had happened as best she could, and she had carried on with her life. She had her job, her friends, and hobbies. She was doing okay, she had learned how to keep those memories and emotions buried. Well, at least throughout the rest of the year, just not at Christmas time.

"I think about it sometimes," she hedged.

"And by sometimes do you mean monthly, weekly, daily, hourly?"

"Not hourly," she said quickly.

"So daily," Brady said grimly. "Ryan's sister-in-law is a psychiatrist, I'll call her in the morning, make you an appointment."

"I don't need a psychiatrist," Aurora protested.

"You do if you still think about what happened every single day. Why didn't you tell me it was that bad?"

Her husband sounded hurt, and that was the last thing she wanted. "I didn't want you to worry."

"And you don't think I'm more worried now finding out you've been hiding this from me?"

"I'm sorry, Brady," she whispered.

"Don't be sorry, just take better care of yourself. We want to start a family one day soon, you need to be taking care of you so you can take care of kids. No more secrets, okay?"

"Okay," she agreed. He was right, if they were going to start trying to get pregnant soon then she couldn't be letting her fears and anxieties get in the way of being the best mother she could be.

"Ready to go up to bed?"

"Not yet." Brady said he wanted honesty so she would give it to him. "Every time I see the Christmas tree I think of that night. I'm back in my brother's house, tied to that chair, with those men threatening me and hurting me, and I..." she trailed off, embarrassed.

"And you want to make some new Christmas tree memories," Brady said, a slow smile breaking out on his handsome face. "I think we can do that. Strip," he ordered playfully, standing her up and taking off his own sweatpants and t-shirt that he slept in.

Aurora did as she was told, her body already warming as thoughts of making love to Brady washed away thoughts of the men who had tried to kill her.

"Lie down on the rug," Brady instructed, his big naked body standing over her.

Again she did as she was told, Brady was always the one in charge in the bedroom, and that was just the way she liked it. She hadn't been very sexually experienced when they met, and she loved that he knew just how to take her body and her mind on a journey into realms of pleasure she would never have even known existed if it wasn't for him.

"I'm going to make sure every time you see a Christmas tree you think of this, and only this," he whispered in her ear.

Then his mouth was crushed against hers, and his hand was between her legs, and he was driving her wild. She writhed and moaned beneath him until he finally gave her what she wanted and plunged deep inside her, joining their bodies together.

Moments later, the world exploded into a mass of sparkly diamond stars.

CHAPTER
Six

December 24th
8:22 A.M.

"Why didn't we clean up last night?" Ashley moaned.

"Because I think *someone* decided they wanted to spend the evening listening to every single Christmas song we could find," Sawyer reminded her, laughing at the pout on her face. After dancing, they'd finished their dinner, and then Ashley had insisted on getting on her phone and finding as many Christmas songs as they could. They had listened to everything from Frosty the Snowman and Rudolph the Red Nosed Reindeer, to O Come All Ye Faithful and Joy to the World, and everything in between. By the time they were done it was after midnight, and they'd both gone up to bed leaving cleaning up the kitchen until morning.

"Why didn't you tell me I was going to regret not helping you clean up and having to do it all today?"

"I'm pretty sure I did," he said, amused. Ashley always hated cleaning up, she avoided it whenever she could, usually causing herself double the work having to do everything in one go.

Sawyer was in a good mood today.

Hanging out with Ashley last night he had come to terms with the idea that they were just going to be friends. He was finally at peace with it. It might not be the way he wished things had turned out, but he hadn't really lost anything, he and Ashley had always been friends. If he could hold her in his arms and slow dance with her then he could do anything. And they had fun together, they really did, last night they had talked and laughed and reminisced about their childhoods. He had a good thing going here, and he was glad he hadn't done anything to mess it up. Who knew maybe soon he'd be ready to date, Morgan Hawksworth was smart and beautiful, and she seemed to like him, maybe in the new year he'd ask her out.

Ashley sighed dramatically as she scrubbed a pot, and he couldn't help but laugh. The only time she was dramatic was when it came to cleaning up.

"So what do you want to do today?" he asked.

"Do you have to cook for tomorrow?"

"Mmhmm, Savannah bakes, I cook. I have to do the turkey, and everyone else is doing the sides."

"What are tomorrow's plans?"

"Savannah and Jett, and Michael, are coming here for lunch, then Samara, Brady and Aurora, Fin and Chloe Patrick with little Asher, are going to join us for dinner. Savannah said Tom, Hannah and Noelle Drake might also stop by if they finish up with their families in time."

"How long does it take to cook the turkey?"

"I have to make the stuffing, then it just goes in the oven for a couple of hours. So whatever you want to do we can."

"I kind of just want to hang out and watch Christmas movies. I'm feeling all Christmassy after last night, and there's not really anything else to do. Everything is decorated, and all my gifts are wrapped, and you only have to cook the turkey, we could light the fire and make s'mores and drink hot chocolate and just watch movies," Ashley said.

"Sounds perfect. How about I finish off the dishes and you go and choose a movie and make the hot chocolate."

"Don't need to tell me twice," Ashley said, setting the pot she'd been scrubbing down and drying her hands on a towel.

Sawyer took over cleaning while Ashley bustled about grabbing things from cupboards. He assumed she was getting snacks, Ashley could never make it through a movie without eating at least three or four different types of snacks.

"I'll go start the fire," he announced when he set the last pot in the dishwasher.

"Okay, I'm almost done," Ashley said.

In the living room, he threw some kindling in the fireplace and lit a match. Once he had a small flame burning he added another couple of sticks and a larger log, and was just standing up when Ashley came bursting in.

"Hot chocolate with little snowmen buddies." She beamed, showing him the mugs.

Sitting inside the mug were little snowmen made out of marshmallows. They had pretzel stick arms, candy corn noses, and little chocolate chip buttons and eyes. "Those are adorable," he said. "And you say you can't cook."

Ashley laughed. "This isn't cooking, all I had to do was stick the marshmallows together, poke holes for the arms and nose and buttons, and melt a little chocolate to draw on the eyes and mouth."

"You melted the chocolate without burning it," he teased.

She rolled her eyes at him. "Be careful, there's a toothpick in the marshmallows," she warned. "I'm going to go upstairs and put my PJs back on, I love watching Christmas movies in my PJs. You shouldn't leave your suit jacket hanging like that on the back of a chair. Want me to take it up for you and put it away in your closet?"

"Yeah, thanks, Ash. I'll grab the cookies, chocolate, and marshmallows for the s'mores, then we can watch a movie. I'll get started on the turkey after that."

It wasn't until Ashley had gone back into the kitchen to grab the jacket that he realized that was a mistake.

The pearls were still in the pocket from last night.

Since he had decided he wasn't going to say anything to Ashley about his feelings they were still in there. He'd forgotten about it, they'd been having too much fun, and then they were both tired so they'd gone straight up to bed. Then this morning they'd had breakfast and cleaned the kitchen, and he'd never thought about the pearls again.

He had to stop her before she picked up the jacket because if she saw the pearls she would know something was going on.

"Actually, Ash, just..." Sawyer trailed off as Ashley came back into the room, his jacket in one hand and the open box with the pearls in the other.

"What's this?" Ashley asked. Her face was a mixture of confusion and suspicion.

"They're pearls," he said a little lamely, mostly because he couldn't think quick enough to come up with an excuse, a plausible reason as to why he—a man—had a set of women's pearls in his jacket pocket, the jacket he'd been wearing when he'd cooked them a romantic, candlelight dinner with all her favorite foods.

"I can see they're pearls." Ashley narrowed her eyes at him. "What are they doing in your pocket?"

Again his brain didn't seem to function, and he couldn't come up with anything smart to stay. He shrugged and said, "I must have put them in there."

"Well, you must have put them in there for a reason. The last time I saw you wear a suit was your sister's wedding. Are these pearls Savannah's?"

"No they aren't."

"Then whose are they?"

"They belonged to my mother."

"Why were they in your jacket?" Ashley asked again. "And don't tell me because you put them there, I'm not an idiot, I know they didn't grow legs and walk in there themselves."

"Of course you're not an idiot," he said quickly. This was quickly spinning out of control. He had just decided to keep his feelings to himself and not ruin the good thing he had going on as Ashley's best friend, and now it seemed he was going to have to tell her anyway.

"Have you been lying to me?" she demanded.

"Lying to you?" He supposed in a way he had. He'd been secretly in love with her since they met and never said anything, which was technically a lie by omission, but the only reason he hadn't said anything was because he hadn't wanted to put Ashley in an awkward position.

"Are you dating someone? Is that why the pearls were in your pocket? Because you were going to give them to your girlfriend?" Ashley's dark eyes were starting to go shimmery as tears built up in them.

"What? No!" he said emphatically. Although he knew he was going to have to move on at some point he wasn't—nor did he want to be—dating anyone else.

"Then what? I don't understand why you would have your mother's pearls in your suit jacket."

Although he had decided he wouldn't do this, it seemed like now he had no choice. He was going to have to tell Ashley the truth and pray that she took it well and this wasn't about to be the end of their friendship.

"I'm not dating anyone," he said. Ashley arched a disbelieving brow. "Really," he added. "I'm not dating anyone. The pearls were in my jacket pocket because I was going to give them to you last night."

"Give them to me?" she asked, confused. "Why were you going to give me your mother's pearls?"

"Because I'm in love with you." He dropped the bombshell.

~

9:06 A.M.

Ashley blinked, sure she must have misheard.

Had Sawyer really just said he was in love with her?

No.

That was ridiculous.

They were friends.

Best friends.

They weren't going to date.

They didn't love each other.

Why was Sawyer saying this?

What was he doing?

He was going to ruin everything.

"Wh-what did you just say?" she stammered. It was a mistake, she was sure that was all it was. She'd misheard, nothing more.

"I said, I'm in love with you," Sawyer repeated miserably, like having this conversation was the last thing he wanted to be doing.

It wasn't like she wanted to be doing it either.

In fact she would rather be doing pretty much anything else.

"You're in love with me?" she asked. It seemed so surreal. If Sawyer was really in love with her then how had she not seen it?

"Yes." He nodded, his blue eyes full of panic like he already knew this wasn't going to go well.

"For how long?" she asked. Was this just some recent development? A product of the two of them living together and spending all day every day together? Because she was guilty of that herself. She'd been lusting after Sawyer these last couple of days, wanting to kiss him, and possibly a whole lot more.

She had even started to realize that what she felt might run deeper than friendship and a bit of lust.

But she had also been smart enough to realize it was a mistake.

You didn't sleep with your best friend.

And if you did you no longer had a best friend.

If they dated and it didn't work out she would be left all alone. There was no way to recover and rebuild their friendship after sex.

Sawyer should know that.

He wasn't an idiot.

So why was he saying these things to her?

"For a long time," Sawyer mumbled an answer to her question.

He was being vague.

Deliberately vague.

He was lying to her again.

"How long is a long time?" Ashley demanded. She wasn't letting Sawyer off the hook, she wanted answers, she wanted to know everything.

"Three years."

Three years?

How was that possible?

"We've known each other for three years," she said.

Sawyer shrugged uncomfortably.

"So you've been in love with me ever since we met and you never said anything?"

Again Sawyer just shrugged.

"This is unbelievable." She rubbed at her temples as though that would help all of this make sense. "Were you ever going to tell me?"

Sawyer met her gaze, and she read in it the answer.

"Of course you were. Last night, that's why you had the pearls in your pocket and cooked that romantic candlelight dinner." Last night at dinner the desire to kiss him had returned but she had quickly squashed it by reminding herself of all the reasons she loved him and of what she had to lose. Little did she know he had wanted to tell her he loved her. "You were going to tell me, but you didn't. Why?"

"Because it was clear you didn't feel the same way."

That wasn't quite true.

There was a very real possibility that she actually did feel the same way as Sawyer, but right now she was too confused and too angry to figure out just what she felt for him.

"This doesn't have to change anything, Ash." Sawyer took a tentative step toward her. "I didn't say anything because I accept that we're always just going to be friends. I'll just deal with my feelings."

"You mean you'll just walk around in love with me but pretending you aren't."

"I'm sorry, Ash," he said helplessly, like he wanted to fix this but didn't know how.

"Why now? Why were you going to tell me now? We've been friends for years. Why did you choose last night to tell me how you felt?"

"Actually, I tried the night before as well but you fell asleep. I don't know why now. I love you, and the last few days we almost kissed twice, and I just, I don't know..." he trailed off.

Those kisses suddenly took on a very different meaning.

No longer were they innocent almost-kisses between two friends who had spent a lot of time together.

Now they felt like manipulations.

Is that what all of this was?

Having her move in, spending all their time together, being so sweet and understanding, doing nice things for her like the fake snow, being a shoulder to cry on, was this just Sawyer trying to get her to be receptive when he dropped his bombshell?

"Nothing has to change, Ash," Sawyer said again.

Was he crazy?

How could anything ever be the same again?

"You're kidding yourself if you think that. Of course things have changed. How could they not? How can I go on being your best friend knowing how you feel?" she demanded.

"I don't know," he said lamely.

She was almost afraid to ask, but she had to know. "Did you use what happened to me to try to get close to me?"

Sawyer's blue eyes widened in shock and hurt filled his face. "Of course not. How could you even think that? I would *never* use the fact that you were raped and nearly murdered for my own ends. You know me, Ashley, you know that's not who I am."

She wanted to believe him.

She really did.

Sawyer had been her rock throughout this whole ordeal, but now it was like someone had dug a huge trench around her then ripped away the rock from underneath her leaving her standing in the middle of a deep hole with no idea how to climb her way back out.

Ashley felt lost and more alone than she had in a long time.

"I don't know anything anymore." She took a deep breath and announced, "I think it's time for me to go back home."

"No," Sawyer said adamantly as though the decision were up to him.

"It's been close to four months now and nothing has happened. I know the killer is still around, I know he's been killing, but he either believes that I'm dead or he just doesn't care. I think after all this time it's safe."

"We don't know that at all. The very fact that he's stayed here and killed two more people without moving on to another city implies he's not finished here. What other reason could that be except you?"

"It could be any number of reasons," she countered. "It was never the plan for me to stay here indefinitely. I'm not going to be stupid about it, I'll ask Brady to install a top of the line security system. I might even get a protection dog. We can ask the local cops to do regular drive-bys just to make sure everything is going okay. I'll be sensible and as safe as I can be, I won't go out alone at night, I'll even get someone to drive me to and from work, but it's time. It's time for me to go back home and it's time for me to go back to living my life. We always knew this day would come, it's just coming a little sooner than we thought."

"I don't want you to go." Sawyer looked devastated, and it took a fair amount of self-control not to go and throw herself in his arms and tell him that she thought she was developing feelings for him too.

But she couldn't.

She felt too betrayed knowing that Sawyer had been lying to her the whole time they'd known each other, and that whether he admitted it or not, he had certainly used what had happened to her to his advantage.

She wasn't saying it was intentional, he might have done it subconsciously, but he'd done it.

"I think it's for the best. I need space, and I need time," she told him.

"So you're not saying this is it?" Sawyer asked hopefully. "Our friendship isn't over?"

"I don't know," she answered honestly. Ashley wanted to tell him what he wanted to hear, but that would be lying. Right now, she didn't know what was going to happen. She didn't know what the future held for them. She didn't want to lose her best friend, but he'd lied to her and taken advantage of her when she was at her most vulnerable, and right now she didn't know how to get past that.

"At least don't go home on your own," Sawyer said, looking defeated. "I'll call Brady, or Michael, one of them can drive you there, check the place out, make sure it's safe. Maybe Michael could even stay with you, just for a few days, until you get the security system and the dog."

Because underneath the hurt she still cared about Sawyer and didn't want him to worry about her, she nodded. "I'll let Brady or Michael drive me home."

This was it.

There was nothing left to say.

It was time.

Although it broke her heart, she set the jacket and the box of pearls down on the nearest piece of furniture and headed for the stairs to go up and pack the few belongings that she had here.

"Goodbye, Sawyer."

"Goodbye, Ashley."

As she started up the stairs, she wondered if those would be the last words they ever spoke to one another.

11:19 A.M.

The house seemed so empty without Ashley in it.

Even though he had been living here for close to five years now and Ashley had only been staying here for the last few months, he had grown accustomed to her presence.

Sawyer kept expecting her to come bouncing down the stairs, or come and sit in the kitchen with him while he cooked the turkey and made the stuffing, or stare out the window complaining about how there was no snow, and it was Christmas Eve and how it didn't feel Christmassy without snow.

But whether it felt like it or not she was definitely gone.

She had packed up her belongings, then gotten into Michael's car, and they had driven away.

It didn't feel real.

Everything had been going so well, they had been having so much fun, and then in one instant, it was all over.

And it was over.

He had to accept that.

He'd seen the look on Ashley's face, she felt betrayed. He had been lying to her the whole time they'd known each other, and she thought that he had taken advantage of her by having her here so he could try to convince her to date him.

That wasn't what he'd done though.

Was it?

Sawyer hadn't thought about it that way, but he supposed if he was objective, he could see how Ashley might interpret it that way.

He felt lost.

He'd stood at the front door staring at the street where Michael's car had disappeared for a solid twenty minutes, then he'd stood and stared at the Christmas tree with all of the gifts Ashley had wrapped sitting underneath for another twenty minutes.

Now he was standing in Ashley's room torturing himself.

Just two nights ago he had slept in here with her when she'd asked him to stay after her nightmare. He had held her in his arms, her warm, soft body snuggled against him, and had the best sleep of his life.

The worst thing about all of this was that he had no one to blame but himself.

If he had just been honest with her months ago, years ago even, or if he had put away his own jacket last night, or said no when she offered to take it upstairs for him, all of this could have been avoided.

"I thought I'd find you up here."

Sawyer whirled around at the voice, startled, he hadn't heard anyone come in, and for a second, he thought it was the killer who had finally managed to track Ashley down. He was ready to pounce on the man and take out all his anger and frustration at losing Ashley.

But then he saw it was just his sister.

"Hey, Sav," he said half-heartedly. He didn't want visitors right now, he just wanted to be alone to wallow in self-pity.

"Jett told me," she said sympathetically. "Do you want to talk about it?"

"No," he said shortly. Talking about it was the last thing he wanted to do right now. It wasn't going to change anything so what was the point?

"Is there anything I can do?" Savannah asked.

He knew his sister just wanted to help. And he knew she had lived out her own worst nightmares several times over with the injuries to her hip and losing Jett, but everything had worked out for her. She might not have the job she had originally wanted thanks to her injury, but she had a job she loved, and she might have missed out on three years with Jett, but they had each other now. He had nothing. The only thing he had ever wanted had just packed her bags and walked out with a finality that said there weren't going to be any second chances.

"Thanks, but there isn't anything anyone can do," he said.

"Is this my fault, Sawyer?" his sister asked anxiously. "The deal we made the other day is that what caused this?"

"No," he replied, deliberately softening his tone. The last thing he wanted was to ruin another Christmas by stressing his sister out thinking she was the cause of Ashley leaving. "Definitely not. This is all on me."

"But the deal, if we hadn't made it then you never would have said anything." Savannah didn't look convinced.

"I didn't say anything. Well, I did, but she was asleep and didn't hear a word I said."

"Then how did she find out?"

"After telling her and her not hearing it, I decided to give it one last try. Last night I cooked her favorite meal, set the table with candles, we both got dressed up, I put on a suit, and Ashley wore this gorgeous black dress. I had mom's pearls, I was going to give them to her. We were eating, and I started to say it, but she started talking about how we're such great friends, and how she wanted us to be friends forever, and how she was afraid of losing me, and I backed out. We spent the night laughing, talking and dancing, and I knew that I would never tell her. I forgot to put the pearls away, and this morning she found them. She knew something was up so I had to tell her everything. She was right, I'd rather have her in my life any way I could. Being friends the rest of our lives was better than this." He waved his hand around indicating the empty bedroom. "Anything is better than this. But it's over. I've lost her. Not only will we never be a couple but now we're not even friends."

"Just give her time, Sawyer." Savannah limped over to stand beside him and put a hand on his arm. "She's dealing with a lot at the moment, and then you tell her something this huge. Knowing that you had been keeping this secret from her for so long upset her, it would have upset me too, but she cares about you and nothing can change that."

Sawyer shook his head. "I don't think so, Sav. She thinks I took advantage of the situation and used having her living here with me to try to get close to her."

"She doesn't, she's just upset and confused."

"She's not. You didn't see her face, you didn't see the way she looked at me. It's over. Really over. And you know what's worse? I think if I had been honest with her from the beginning I actually had a chance with her. If I'd asked her out I think she would have said yes. So I have no one to blame for this mess but myself."

"I'm sorry, Sawyer. I really am. If Ashley isn't smart enough to see what an amazing guy you are and how happy you would make her then she doesn't deserve you. There's someone out there for you, and now that you finally have closure maybe you can move on."

Maybe.

But he doubted it.

At least not for a while.

Someday he might be in a place where he could start dating but that day wasn't today, and it wasn't tomorrow, and it wasn't any time soon.

His life might be falling apart, but his sister's wasn't. "I'm sorry, Sav, I haven't even congratulated you properly yet. I'm so thrilled that you and Jett are having a baby." Sawyer wrapped his arms around his sister and squeezed her tightly, he knew how excited she must be, and he didn't want her tapering it down for his benefit.

"Thanks." She wrapped her arms around him and squeezed back. "Just give it some time. Let her process everything, I think she'll come around. Jett and I will have Christmas lunch and dinner at our house tomorrow so you don't have to worry about having everyone over."

Christmas.

Celebrating the holiday of love, and joy, and peace, and miracles was the last thing he wanted to be doing right now.

"I can still do the turkey if you want," he offered.

"It's fine, Jett said he'd help me tonight."

"Aren't you supposed to be baking your gingerbread creation tonight?"

"Jett and I will be busy." Savannah grinned, it was clear she couldn't wait to start baking. "But I'm all yours for now. Want to go and watch The Santa Clause?"

Although he wanted to forget all about Christmas he didn't want to dampen Savannah's mood. "Sure. So what theme is your gingerbread creation this year?" he asked as they headed back downstairs to the living room.

"A nursery." Savannah beamed.

He laughed despite himself. "I can't wait to see that."

"Last Christmas I thought Jett and I were completely over. I was stuck in my wheelchair because I was too afraid to try getting up and walking. I got my Christmas miracle, Sawyer, so don't give up hope, you never know, you might get yours too."

As much as he wished that was true, he knew it wasn't. He looked down at the two mugs of hot chocolate on the table, the ones Ashley had made earlier with the adorable little marshmallow snowmen.

With everything that had gone on he'd forgotten about them.

Having sat in the hot liquid too long, the marshmallows had melted.

The sticky, sugary substance was now half hanging off the toothpick and half dissolved in the now cold hot chocolate.

The pretzel arms and candy corn nose floated alongside the smooshy marshmallow.

Those little ruined snowmen were an exact representation of how he was feeling right now—broken, destroyed, with parts of him fallen off.

The snowmen couldn't be put back together, and neither could his Christmas or his life.

There weren't going to be any Christmas miracles for him.

~

1:26 P.M.

All these months she had been dying to come back home and resume her normal life, but now that she was here, it wasn't anything like she'd thought it would be.

She felt so alone.

Ashley hadn't realized just how comfortable she had become at Sawyer's house until she left.

Now she wished she hadn't.

Maybe.

Or not.

She wasn't really sure.

She was so confused.

Had she made the right decision moving out?

She wasn't worried about the killer, Samara and Aurora were coming over soon, and then Brady would be joining them tonight, they were going to have kind of a Christmassy sleepover. Ashley really wasn't in the mood, she would rather be alone, but it was nice that her friends cared enough to be there for her, and it meant she wouldn't be alone in the event the killer had been watching her house.

She was worried that things had become such a mess between her and Sawyer and her moving out had only compounded them to the point they could never be fixed.

Sawyer was in love with her.

Wasn't that what she wanted?

She was attracted to Sawyer, and over the last couple of days she had begun to realize that she felt something for him beyond friendship, so she liked him, and he liked her. What was the problem?

She was afraid.

That was the problem.

Right now she just wasn't sure that she could risk losing the person she loved most in the world. What would she do without Sawyer? If they dated and then broke up they could never go back to being best friends. They'd no doubt try, but it wouldn't last, things would be awkward, and over time they would drift apart.

And yet hadn't she lost him anyway?

She had walked away because she was angry about him lying, and hurt because it felt like he had taken advantage of her when she was at her most vulnerable.

Or if she was being a little more honest, she had walked away because she was afraid.

Afraid of losing what she had already given up.

Ashley was so confused. She wasn't sure this was what she wanted, she wasn't sure what the best thing to do was, and she was getting tired of trying to figure it out. She was hurt and angry, and for now, she just needed a break.

It wasn't like she had to figure this out today, she had plenty of time to sort out her feelings and what she wanted. Maybe taking a break from spending time with Sawyer was just what she needed. Space would help her see things clearly and give her time for her emotions to settle down so she didn't say or do something she'd later regret.

The doorbell rang, and she roused herself off the couch and stumbled toward the door.

"Hey, guys." She smiled when she opened the door.

"We come with gifts," Aurora said, holding a plate piled high with Christmas goodies she was sure had come from Savannah.

"And a tree," Samara added, a hand on a Christmas tree that balanced against the wall.

"We thought we'd spend the day decorating, if we're spending the night here it has to be Christmassy," Aurora said.

While it wasn't how she wanted to spend her Christmas Eve it would help to keep her distracted. At least she hoped it would. Either that or it would just remind her of decorating Sawyer's house a couple of weeks ago.

"I'll help with the tree," Ashley said.

Together she and Samara lugged the tree down the hall and into the living room, setting it up over by the window in the corner.

"Here will do," she said. "I like the way the lights glow in the window."

"So, what's up with you and Sawyer?" Aurora asked.

So much for a distraction.

It seemed like instead of coming to hang out with her and decorate, they were really here to grill her for information.

"Brady said that you and Sawyer had a fight, but he didn't give any details," Aurora added, taking a seat on the couch.

"We don't want to pry," Samara said, sitting beside Aurora.

"But we do want to help," Aurora added.

Ashley sighed, as much as she didn't want to talk about it maybe her friends could help her get some perspective. That was what friends were for wasn't it? To help you out when you needed someone, to bounce ideas off, to give you perspective. That was what Sawyer always did, but Sawyer wasn't here right now, and he was the one she needed advice about.

"Did you two know that he's been in love with me practically since we met?" She wondered whether she was the only one in the dark about Sawyer's feelings or if he'd been able to hide them from everyone.

Her friends exchanged glances, then Samara said, "We didn't *know,* but we did suspect."

"So, I was the only one who didn't see it."

"I guess so," Aurora said.

"And none of you thought to mention this to me?" she demanded. If everyone seemed to know that Sawyer liked her then why hadn't they clued her in?

"We thought you knew," Samara replied.

"How can I know if no one tells me?" she snapped, then immediately felt bad. It wasn't Samara and Aurora she was angry with, and she shouldn't be taking out her frustrations on them. Ashley sunk on the sofa beside her friends. "Sorry, it's just I nearly died, and then I've lived knowing someone wants me dead for months now, and Sawyer had been my rock, and now he's not, and it's Christmas, and everything is supposed to be happy and perfect but it's not, it's the opposite, and there isn't even any snow," she finished miserably.

"Jett and Morgan will find Evander Hurley," Aurora said confidently. "So that problem will soon be taken care of. And the problem with Sawyer is only a problem if you don't like him. *Do* you like him?"

Ashley hesitated, not quite sure how to answer that. "I don't know. If you'd asked me that even just a month ago I would have said no of course not we're just friends, best friends, but the last few days I've been seeing him differently. A couple of times I even wanted to kiss him," she admitted.

"You like him," Aurora and Samara declared in unison.

"Maybe, but it doesn't matter, he lied to me—every single day for more than three years.

"Sometimes you keep things from the people you love because you think it's for the best," Aurora said quietly, in such a way it was clear she was talking about herself and Brady as well as Sawyer.

"He could have told me," she insisted.

"He was probably afraid of losing you as a friend," Samara said. "But he likes you and you like him, so what's the problem?"

"Yeah, what's the problem?" Aurora echoed. "Sawyer has to be one of the best catches around. He's sweet, thoughtful, kind, and have you seen his body? It's to die for. And more importantly, you know that he loves you and would do anything for you. Isn't that exactly what you want in a guy?"

"It is," she reluctantly agreed.

"Then why are you here and not back at Sawyer's?" Samara asked.

"Because I'm afraid," she admitted quietly.

"Of what?' Aurora asked.

"I've always been the strong one. When my mom was sick all those times I never let her see me cry, I was always positive even when I didn't feel like being upbeat. I was strong for my mom and for my dad, even after mom died, my dad needed me to be strong. And these last few months everything has been so messed up except for Sawyer. He's been amazing. More than amazing, he's been perfect. What would I do if we dated and then broke up and I lost him?"

"It's okay to be afraid, Ash," Aurora said, taking her hand and squeezing. "And there's nothing wrong with crying and not always being strong and in control. You don't have to keep up a front for us or for Sawyer. But you can't let fear stop you from living your life. How would you feel if Sawyer moved on and you lost your chance with him?"

She knew exactly how she'd feel.

She would feel just like she'd felt when she'd found those pearls in Sawyer's jacket, and she thought he was dating someone and hadn't told her.

She'd felt like she had lost a piece of herself.

"I think your face says it all," Aurora said with a smile. "You'd be devastated. Don't let what-ifs ruin what could be. If you need a few days then take them, then sit down with Sawyer and talk this out. Don't let him slip away because you know you'll regret it if you do."

Aurora was right.

If she let Sawyer get away just because she was afraid and annoyed that he'd lied to her then she would regret it, and she had promised her mother on her death bed that she wouldn't live a life of regrets.

"Okay," she agreed.

"Great." Aurora beamed. "Now, I'm starving. Have you had lunch?"

"Nope, I didn't have breakfast either."

"How about we order pizza, it should be here by the time we bring up all the boxes of decorations from the basement," Samara suggested.

"Sounds like a plan," Ashley agreed. "I don't know where everything is down in the basement, it might take us a while to find the boxes."

"Samara and I packed everything up when you moved in with Sawyer, we should be able to find everything pretty easily," Aurora said.

"Thanks for being here," she said to her friends, she really was very lucky to have people who loved and cared about her.

"That's what we're here for," Samara said.

"Now let's go get those decorations and turn this place into a Christmassy wonderland," Aurora said.

A Christmassy wonderland, that was exactly what she needed right now, something beautiful and fun in her life, then maybe after Christmas she'd be able to see if she and Sawyer could also have something beautiful together.

❧

1:55 P.M.

He had her.

After all those months of patiently and painstakingly watching and waiting, he finally had her.

Evander didn't think he had stopped grinning ever since he realized he was finally going to get his wish, he was finally going to finish what he started, he was finally going to claim Ashley Fallon as his next kill.

He had done it. With the help of the drone he had managed to track down the house where Ashley had been hiding out. Although he knew it was risky to keep using the drone after the sun rose he had told himself just one more street, and then he'd stop for the day.

It was the eighth house on the block.

The drone had been hovering at the back window when the little camera he'd fitted to it had relayed images back to him of Ashley and the man from the park washing dishes in the kitchen. As tempting as it was to go running straight in there he knew the man was armed so he knew he had to play it smart.

Before he'd had a chance to come up with a plan the universe had once again taken a hand in helping him play out his revenge.

Ashley had left the house with a bag in tow. She had gotten into a car with a different man, and they'd driven back to her house.

Evander didn't have to get close enough to this new man to know he would also be armed. Perhaps the man Ashley had been staying with was a bodyguard. It made sense. Although they had faked her death, they also had to know that he would know he hadn't been in Ashley's hospital room long enough to kill her so their ruse might not work. They also knew that he was resourceful, he'd tracked her down at the hospital, he could do it again. Having her stay with a bodyguard meant that even if he did manage to find her getting to her would be a different story.

And it *did* present a challenge.

A bodyguard would be armed and trained, and would do whatever necessary to protect their charge.

He was going to have to be very careful.

At least that's what he'd thought.

But then the man who had driven Ashley back to her house had left. Again he had been about to go inside and finally finish what he'd started, but a car had pulled up, a different one this time, and two young women had gotten out, with a Christmas tree, and Ashley had let them in.

Three women.

Three beautiful, dark-haired women.

This was going to turn out even better than he could have ever hoped for. Not only was he finally going to be able to kill Ashley Fallon, but her two dark-haired friends as well. Three for the price of one.

The universe really loved him.

Evander didn't think he could kill someone who didn't look like Petunia Smith. Because killing someone who didn't look like her would be like he wasn't really killing Petunia, so what was the point of that?

It was Petunia Smith that he hated.

It was Petunia Smith who had ruined his life.

It was Petunia Smith who he wished he could wrap his hands around her neck and squeeze and squeeze until he squeezed the life right out of her.

Like every other kid in their junior class, he had a crush on Petunia. That long silky dark hair, those soulful black eyes, that milky white skin, she was like some kind of sexy Snow White.

But like most of the boys in their class, he knew she was so far out of his league that there was no point in even asking her out.

He was a geek.

She was a goddess.

She would never even look at him.

Until one day she had.

It was like a dream.

She'd walked up to him at their lockers, which just so happened to be side by side. She had looked up at him with a shy smile and introduced herself. She had said that she thought he was cute and whispered that she wanted to meet him in the boys' bathroom after school.

That should have been his first clue.

Girls like that didn't ask boys like him to meet in the bathroom to make out.

But he was young and stupid and like all teenage boys, full of hormones. Being the geek that he had been back then he had never had a girlfriend, he barely even had friends. He hadn't even kissed a girl before.

All the rest of the day, he had thought of nothing else but meeting Petunia in the bathroom. He had run scenarios in his mind about exactly how it would all play out. She would tell him she was secretly in love with him, he would admit he'd had a crush on her since their freshman year. Then they would kiss, maybe she'd even let him touch her breasts, or if he was really lucky, they'd have sex. The bathroom wasn't the most romantic place for a first time, but at least it would be a first time.

Only that wasn't what had happened.

It wasn't even close.

As soon as school was over, he'd all but run straight to the bathroom, where he'd had to wait close to thirty minutes for Petunia. He had thought she wasn't coming, been all prepared to leave, had felt like such a fool for thinking someone like her could like someone like him, he had even almost cried.

But then she'd come.

Her long hair flowing around her shoulders, her dark eyes sparkling, dressed in a skimpy bright red dress that barely covered everything.

Petunia had told him that she'd been held up trying to get rid of her boyfriend, and was so glad he was still there waiting for her.

Then she'd said the words he had never thought he would hear.

She had asked him to strip and lay his clothes out on the floor like a blanket so they wouldn't have to have sex on the dirty bathroom floor.

He hadn't had to be asked twice.

He had complied immediately.

The second he was naked she had grabbed his clothes, pulled out her phone, and started filming him, laughing the whole time.

Then the door had been thrown open, and Petunia's boyfriend had been there, laughing and taunting him, while he had stood there and cried.

Those laughs still echoed in his head.

As if that wasn't bad enough, that video had been sent to every single kid who attended their school.

He attempted suicide the next day.

Wrapped a metal chain around his neck and tried to hang himself.

His father found him, got him down, and rushed him to the hospital. He was committed to a psychiatric facility, Petunia Smith and her boyfriend were expelled, but no legal action was taken. His parents sued her on his behalf, and he was awarded a fairly large sum of money.

But what good was money?

His life had already been ruined.

He might have lived, but a part of him had died in that bathroom and would never come back.

Instead, the beast had grown inside him, screaming for its own form of revenge.

Petunia had deprived him of that by dying before he could be the one to take her life from her.

So he had found an alternative.

After being humiliated the way he had, Evander had never been able to have sex. He'd had a girlfriend while he was in college, she'd liked him, she'd gladly come into his bed, but when it was time to perform, he couldn't. It had been humiliating, and he had ended the relationship immediately. Petunia's hold on him remained strong. Even after he had worked hard to build muscles on his skinny body, and found a way to make money from what he had gone through so he could buy himself everything his heart desired.

Unfortunately, revenge couldn't be bought.

The only way he could sleep with a woman was to rape them and then kill them so they—and he in a way—didn't have to live with what he had done.

It was a system that had worked up until Ashley Fallon.

She had almost slipped through his fingers, but now he was here, standing outside her house, ready to go in and make not one but three kills.

Maybe it was wrong for him to kill, perhaps it was wrong for him to seek revenge when the person who had hurt him had suffered her own sort of punishment, but he didn't care.

None of this was his fault.

His life had been ruined.

A beast, born of revenge, now controlled him.

Once he may have been a weak, helpless boy, so desperate to fit in and be accepted he would do anything, but now he was a strong, fierce warrior fighting for the justice he deserved.

A pizza delivery truck pulled up in the driveway, another sign the universe was pleased with his self-help method of rebuilding his life.

Evander jogged over to the pizza guy. "How much do I owe you?" he asked.

The young man didn't even blink, just rattled off an amount, took the money Evander gave him, jumped in his car, and drove off.

As much as he would have liked to take his time with Ashley, he had no idea when one of the men he believed to be bodyguards would return. That they *would* return was a given.

He was going to have to make this quick, but it would still be fun.

~

2:02 P.M.

"Why do you have so many Christmas decorations?" Samara asked as she picked up another box and carried it over to the bottom of the basement steps to join the other eleven boxes.

Ashley giggled. "Because you can never have too many Christmas decorations."

"How many of them are snowman ones?" Aurora asked.

"Umm," Ashley said with a laugh, "possibly a few."

"Like all of them?" Samara asked. She'd always wished there was something she loved like Ashley loved snowmen, but there wasn't. Her life before 'the incident' as it was always referred to, she was too busy being bounced around and dealing with her feelings of being unwanted, and life after 'the incident' she had been too busy trying to make up for what she had done to have time for anything else.

"Pretty much," Ashley replied, looking happier now. Her eyes were shining, her cheeks were tinted pink, and her smile and her laugh sounded natural and easy. It looked like their talk about Sawyer had helped her find the answers she needed.

Samara wished her problems could be solved so simply.

But some things, once you'd done them, could never be taken back.

No amount of giving herself permission to take a few days and then push her fears aside and go after what she wanted was going to work for her.

She had a lot to make up for, a lot to try and make right, and she would do it, even if it took every second of her life.

She *would* make it right.

"I think there are only another couple of boxes then we can take them upstairs and start decorating," Aurora said. Her other friend sounded bouncy and upbeat today as well. She knew Christmas time was a mixed bag of emotions for Aurora given what she had lived through on Christmas Eve a couple of years ago, and she knew that Aurora had been struggling with those emotions, but had been hesitant to tell her husband about it. From the smile on her face this morning, Samara guessed that Aurora and Brady had finally talked and it had gone better than Aurora had been expecting.

It seemed like everyone was getting what they wanted this Christmas except her.

Samara wished that one day she might get her own Christmas miracle.

Having the weight of trying to make amends for past mistakes was crushing her.

"By the time we get the boxes up—" Ashley broke off as the door-bell rang. "I was just going to say by the time we got the boxes up the pizza should be here but looks like that's it."

"I'll go grab it," Samara offered. "You two find the last boxes then we'll carry them up and eat."

Leaving her friends in the basement, Samara headed upstairs, trying to muster up some Christmassy enthusiasm. She had never enjoyed the holidays, it was hard to enjoy a time of year that was meant to be about hope, and joy, and love, when no one wanted you.

Grabbing her purse from the small table in the hall, she punched in the alarm code and pulled out her wallet as she opened the door to find a man with a pizza box and a knife standing on the doorstep.

She opened her mouth to scream, but the man moved too quickly.

Before she could draw in air and start screaming the man had tossed the pizza at her, causing her to stumble backward, then he lunged toward her, wrapping an arm around her neck and yanking her up against his body.

The tip of the knife hovered above her left eye, and he whispered in her ear, "It's a pity you have blue eyes and not brown, but I could always cut them out, then it wouldn't matter." He laughed like it was the funniest thing ever, then closed and locked the door.

Samara wasn't sure what she should do.

She had no doubt that this was the killer that wanted Ashley dead.

He had obviously tracked her down and either hadn't been fooled by the ruse that Ashley was dead, or had been staking out the house and seen her come home.

While they had always known that was a possibility, Jett and Morgan had been confident that the man wouldn't do anything if Ashley wasn't alone, which was why she and Aurora were here, and why they, and Brady, would be spending the night.

Jett and Morgan were obviously wrong.

The killer had grown more daring, and she had no doubt that he would kill her and Aurora as well as Ashley.

"Where are the others?" the man hissed.

If she was going to die she wasn't taking the others down with her.

Samara clamped her lips together.

"I don't have time for games." With that, he plunged the knife into her arm, the one that had instinctively risen to try to claw at the arm crushing her airway.

Blood immediately began to flow from the wound, and the accompanying pain brought tears to her eyes, but she wasn't going to tell him what he wanted to know. Although there were three of them to his one, with her as a hostage, they wouldn't be able to use that to their advantage. They were basically sitting ducks.

She was sure that sooner rather than later Brady would call to check on Aurora. And she hadn't reset the alarm. The whole security system wasn't set up yet, but Brady had managed to call in a couple of favors to get something basic set up even if it was Christmas Eve. The security system was linked to the firm's system and should send an alert to Brady's phone.

But this man seemed to know that he had to be quick, so Samara wasn't sure help would arrive in time.

"Ah, never mind, the basement I suspect," he said, nodding at the open door.

Dragging her with him he crossed the room, and as soon as they reached the top of the basement stairs, she could hear her friends' laughing, happy voices.

"Hello, ladies," Evander said cheerfully as they descended the steps.

Both Ashley and Aurora froze, their heads whipping in hers and Evander's direction. Their eyes grew wide when they saw the knife at her throat and the blood on her arm.

Even though she couldn't see his face, Samara could hear the smirk in Evander Hurley's voice when he spoke. "You do anything stupid, and she loses an eye. The blue eyes ruin things anyway so I don't mind doing it, but I'm trying to be nice."

"H-how did you find me?" Ashley stammered.

"Persistence. And luck," Evander answered. "You practically fell into my lap at the park the other morning. You got away, but I knew you had to be somewhere close by. I found the house you'd been hiding out in and followed you back here."

"Why can't you just let me go?" Ashley pleaded.

"Because Petunia got away, I'm not letting that happen again."

Samara had no idea who Petunia was, she didn't care about Evander Hurley's backstory, all she cared about was staying alive.

"I didn't come prepared for three pretty girls, so we're going to have to improvise." Evander spun her around as he obviously scanned the room looking for something to use, for what she wasn't quite sure, but she knew it was for nothing good. "Ah, Christmas lights. Perfect."

What was he going to do with the Christmas lights?

"Just let my friends go," Ashley begged. "They don't have anything to do with this."

"They do now. They've seen my face, and besides they're pretty, they look like Petunia, and the beast is hungry."

She had no idea what this beast was Evander was talking about, but she suspected it was how he justified murdering women.

"You," Evander nodded at Aurora, "take this and tie Ashley's hands behind her back."

When Aurora hesitated, Evander scraped the tip of his knife along the skin just under Samara's eye. She tried to hold it in, but a small, terrified, pained moan escaped.

The sound was enough to spur Aurora into action, and she picked up the rope Evander had thrown to her and tied it around Ashley's wrists.

Samara couldn't see a way they were walking out of this alive.

As long as Evander had the knife and clearly wasn't afraid to use it, they were helpless. She knew her friends wouldn't do anything to risk her getting hurt, but she would gladly sacrifice herself for them. They had hope for their futures. She had nothing.

Evander yanked her sideways and bent, opening one of the boxes and pulling out a long string of Christmas lights. Without moving the knife more than an inch from her eye he wrapped one end of the string tightly around her neck.

Her hands flew to her neck, trying to claw at the string to loosen it enough that she could breathe.

He dragged her over to the middle of the room and threw the other end of the Christmas lights over a pipe that ran along the ceiling. Evander took the other end and called to Aurora, "Come over here like a good girl so I don't have to hurt your friend again." To emphasize his point he lazily trailed the knife down her cheek, just hard enough to scratch the skin.

With a defeated sigh Aurora stepped closer, and Evander yanked her over and tied the other end of the string around her neck as well.

"So very festive of me." Evander grinned, standing back to admire his handiwork.

Stretched out as it was over the pipe, the Christmas lights were only just long enough to wrap around their necks and leave them both balancing on their tiptoes. If Samara lowered her heels to the floor then the string would tighten around Aurora's neck and strangle her, the same would happen to her if Aurora moved.

"I'll be back for you two later, but for now Ashley and I have a little unfinished business."

～

2:31 P.M.

. . .

He should get in his car and drive to Ashley's.

No.

He should stay here, leave well enough alone, not make things worse.

No.

He should check on her, apologize again.

No.

He should give her some space and time.

No.

He should make sure she was safe, a killer was after her.

No.

He should wait until she was ready to see him.

Sawyer had been having the same debate with himself ever since Ashley had left. He wanted to do the right thing he just wasn't sure what that was. He loved Ashley, and he couldn't just turn off his protective instincts where she was concerned. But at the same time, he didn't want to just turn up there and make her more angry with him than she already was.

And she was pretty angry with him.

He felt like such an idiot. He had let fear dictate his actions, and instead of avoiding a catastrophe he had all but invited it to come knocking at his door.

Because of that decision Ashley wasn't here, safe and protected, where he could look after her. Instead, she was at her house, vulnerable, should the killer be keeping tabs on her. Yes, he knew that Brady had gotten part of the security system installed, and yes, he knew that Aurora and Samara were there and that so far the killer only targeted women when they were alone. Yes, he knew that Brady would be spending the night there, but none of those things made him feel any better.

It wasn't that he didn't trust other people to keep her safe it was just that...

He didn't trust other people to keep her safe.

He wanted to be with her.

No one loved her like he did, so no one could keep her safe like he could.

"She'll be fine," Brady said.

"Easy for you to say," he muttered. It wasn't the woman Brady loved in danger, it was the woman *he* loved in danger.

"Do you think I would have let Aurora stay at that house if I thought Evander was going to go after Ashley today?" Brady asked.

Sawyer arched a blond brow. "*Let her*? You say that kind of stuff in front of your wife?" He tried to lighten his mood by making a joke.

"Nope, I'm not crazy, I want to live," Brady joked back. "But seriously, Sawyer, even if Evander knows she's still alive, and even if he knows where she lives, and even if he knows she's back there, I don't think he's going to do anything so long as she's not alone. Plus there's an alarm there now. Aurora, Ashley, and Samara all know to keep the alarm armed and not let anyone in."

That should reassure him but it didn't.

The only thing that was going to ease his concerns was seeing Ashley with his own two eyes, and that was out of the question.

"Want me to go over there and check on her?" Michael asked. If anyone understood unrequited love it was Michael. He knew that his friend had a crush on Samara Patrick, and that although he and Samara were friends there didn't appear to be any hope of them ever moving out of the friend zone. Sawyer hoped things worked out better for Michael and Samara than they had for him and Ashley.

"Thanks, but I think she'd know you were just there because of me." Sawyer paused, tried to make the choice that would be what Ashley wanted. Couldn't. Then said, "Maybe wait another thirty minutes and then go over there."

"Deal." Michael smiled, and Sawyer assumed he wanted to go over there to check on Samara as much as to be a good friend and check on Ashley.

Sawyer was about to say something when there was a knock on his door.

Although he knew Ashley would be fine, and it had only been a couple of hours since Michael had seen her he couldn't help but get the feeling this was going to be bad news.

From the look on both Brady and Michael's faces, they had the same feeling in their gut that he had.

He opened the door to find Jett and Morgan standing there.

His stomach plummeted.

"Is it Ashley? Did something happen to her?" he asked, the words chasing themselves out of his mouth and coming out in one long blur.

"Not as far as I know," Jett replied.

"Isn't Ashley still here?" Morgan asked.

"No, she left this morning. Michael took her back home. She decided it had been nearly four months and no signs of the killer coming after her and it was safe enough for her to go home."

"You two have a fight?" Jett asked sympathetically.

Sawyer shrugged and led them into the living room. Going over and over the fight and the events leading up to it were only making him more on edge. He had to let it go, give Ashley some time, and who knows, maybe Savannah was right, and with time and space she might come round.

"What are you guys doing here?" Brady asked. "It's Christmas Eve, aren't you going home and leaving this case until after the holidays?"

"We were going to go home at lunchtime, but then we got a phone call," Morgan explained.

"About Ashley's case? About Evander Hurley?" he asked. He would love if this case was over before tomorrow so Ashley could enjoy her Christmas without a death sentence hanging over her head.

"Maybe, we're not sure but we think it could be. That's why we came," Jett said. "We were wondering if he managed to find your house."

"You think he knows this is where Ashley was staying?" If Evander thought Ashley was here then for the moment at least she was safe.

"There was a call to the local cops this morning that was forwarded on to us because we asked to be notified of any unusual activity in your street and Ashley's," Jett said.

"What did the call say?" Sawyer wanted to grab hold of the FBI agents and shake them until information fell out. Didn't they know this was hell for him? Jett should know what he was going through, he knew what it was like when his crazy ex-partner threatened Savannah.

"Someone reported a drone outside their window last night," Morgan informed him.

"A drone?" That sounded like it could be anything.

"A drone," Morgan nodded.

"We're not saying this has anything to do with Evander Hurley and Ash, but a few days ago there was someone in the park when Ashley fell down that hill, and now someone is flying drones in your street. Maybe it's just an early Christmas gift someone was playing with, or something else, but we can't be too careful. Have you noticed anything unusual?" Jett asked.

"No, nothing springs to mind, although," he said thoughtfully, "last night Ashley was outside and she thought she saw something. She said it was like light reflecting off something metallic, that could have been a drone. She called out, and I went outside, we saw a balloon with a little box of dolls attached, it belonged to the Wilkins kids, but it could have been a drone."

"If he knows that Ashley was staying here then he could have been watching the house," Morgan said.

Which meant the killer could have seen Ashley leave.

He could have followed Michael's car back to Ashley's house.

He could be there right now.

And Ashley was alone with Samara and Aurora, and while he liked both women, neither of them was trained or armed.

Apparently Brady was worried about that as well because he pulled out his phone and tapped away on it.

The color drained from Brady's face.

That wasn't good.

"What?" he demanded.

"The alarm for the house was disarmed about thirty minutes ago, but it was never rearmed," Brady said tightly.

That was all Sawyer needed to hear.

His body was already moving before his brain even processed what he was doing.

"We can't just go running blindly in there," Jett said.

"What do you suggest we do, sit around and have a meeting about it? He could be there, right now, inside her house. He's waited over three months for this, if he's been watching then he has to know we're armed. He's not stupid, he stayed under the radar for three years before he started making mistakes, he's going to move quickly."

As was he.

Sawyer was already pulling his gun from the safe in the hall and heading for his car.

This wasn't the time to stand around and talk.

The only time they had to figure out a plan would be the ten minutes it took to drive from his house to Ashley's.

Both Brady and Michael were right on his heels as they all climbed into Jett and Morgan's car since it was the one closest to the street.

He wasn't the only one with a vested interest here.

All three of them had people they loved in that house.

Sawyer prayed that no one was going to lose their other half this Christmas Eve.

Christmas was supposed to be a time for miracles, and they needed a big one.

~

2:41 P.M.

Ashley wanted to run.

Try to get help.

But she was afraid if she did anything to make Evander angry he was going to take it out on Aurora or Samara.

He already had them basically suspended from the ceiling with a string of Christmas lights tied around each of their necks. They were both balancing precariously on their tiptoes so the cord didn't cut off their air supply, but she wasn't sure how long they could maintain that position. Particularly Samara, whose arm was still gushing blood that was puddling beneath her on the concrete floor of the basement.

She was never going to look at Christmas lights the same way again.

"Either of you two even think of screaming, and I'll make sure your little friend here suffers before I kill her," Evander warned Aurora and Samara.

Then Evander wrapped a hand around her arm and began to drag her up the stairs. Ashley looked back, caught her friends' eyes, this could be the last time she ever saw them. They could be the last people other than Evander she ever saw.

It was hard to walk with her hands tied behind her back and Evander yanking her along. His legs were longer than hers, and he kept making her trip, her shins banging painfully against the steps.

She hoped help was coming.

Brady was supposed to be coming after lunch, and it was approaching three o'clock, surely he should be here soon. And if she knew Sawyer—and she did—he would send Michael over here at some point to check up on her.

Ashley had hoped that her coming back here would bring Evander out of hiding, she had just hoped it would happen when she had some backup.

It wasn't that she wanted to play bait, well not exactly, but one of the reasons she had wanted to come back here was to draw Evander out. If she had lost her rock when she learned about Sawyer's feelings for her then she needed to get her footing back somehow. She needed the threat hanging over her to be gone. And as much as she needed space from Sawyer, part of her wanting to come back here was definitely the hope that Evander couldn't resist taking another shot at her and that in doing so he would get himself caught.

But she hadn't wanted him to come like this.

Not when she was here with her friends who were now going to die because of her. She had thought she'd have some time to talk with Jett and Morgan about setting some sort of trap, she had thought she'd have at least until after the holidays.

Now it was too late.

Too late for a lot of things.

Including her and Sawyer.

Ashley wished she had decided not to wait a couple of days before talking to Sawyer. She had thought that a few days, a bit of space, would be just what they needed, then they could sit down and talk things through when they weren't both so hopped up on emotion.

But now she had missed her chance.

"Hey." Evander shook her, and she blinked and realized that he had dragged her all the way up the stairs and managed to locate her bedroom. "I'm speaking to you, pay attention."

She didn't want to pay attention.

Who wanted to pay attention to their own death?

She wanted to find some quiet, peaceful place in her mind to crawl into so that she didn't have to know what was happening.

No, that wasn't quite true.

What she *really* wanted to do was fight back.

She wanted to take Evander's knife and shove it into his heart.

She wanted him to die, not just for what he had done to her, or what he was going to do to her and her friends, but for the eighteen women he had killed and their families who would forever have a piece missing.

"You've been a long time coming, and you're not ruining this for me," Evander said as he tossed her onto her bed. With her wrists bound behind her back she landed awkwardly, and pain zipped up to her shoulders and back down again to her fingers.

Ashley saw only two options to survive.

The first was to wait for help to arrive. She was positive that sooner or later someone was going to come, either Brady, or Michael, or maybe even Sawyer. If she could get Evander talking, stall things, then there was a chance, however slim, that she wasn't going to die this Christmas Eve.

The second was to take matters into her own hands. If she wanted to live she couldn't rely on anyone else. Someone was coming, and she may be able to stall until they got here, but they could come too late.

But she had an ace up her sleeve that Evander didn't know about.

When Aurora had tied the rope around her wrists, she had done it so her palms were together and tucked the ends of the rope between them. That meant there was a chance that she could untie herself. All she needed was enough of a distraction, and getting Evander talking should do that.

Drawing in a deep breath, she had nothing to lose after all. "Who was Petunia?"

Evander scowled at her.

It was terrifying to be so close to the face that had haunted her every day since the first of September when her life had been forever changed. Although she had always known he would almost definitely come back for her if he got another chance, part of her had never believed it would actually happen. Ashley didn't think it was coming back here that had been her mistake, it was not making a plan with Jett and Morgan to use that to their advantage. It was stupid of all of them not to, but no one thought he'd come after her unless she was alone.

They had underestimated Evander.

Underestimated just how desperate he was.

She wasn't going to make that mistake again.

Evander was ranting away, she didn't bother listening, she didn't care who Petunia was or what she'd done to Evander, all she cared about was living to spend Christmas with Sawyer. Because if she made it out of this alive the first thing she was doing was sorting out their relationship.

Working the ropes was hard, her hands were behind her and pressed between her body and the mattress, making it even harder, but giving up wasn't an option. Not when her life and Aurora and Samara's were at stake. Holding one end of the rope still, she pushed the other end toward the knot, hoping to loosen it a little, all while trying not to move so Evander didn't figure out what she was doing. Aurora hadn't done the knot particularly tightly, and Evander hadn't bothered to check, just tied up Aurora and Samara, and dragged her up here. He knew he had to move quickly and it had made him sloppy, to her benefit.

It didn't take long before she felt the rope begin to loosen.

Ashley almost squealed in delighted relief, but managed to clamp her lips together, she couldn't ruin things when she was so close.

Now it was time to tune Evander's ramblings back in, she needed to make her timing perfect down to the exact second. If she messed this up she was a dead woman. He still had the knife, and she was unarmed.

"Petunia didn't die at my hands, but I can still take solace in the knowledge that I made her last months on earth a living hell. Kind of like I did for you." Evander grinned at her.

In a way what he'd just said was true, but in another way, he'd actually given her Sawyer. If she hadn't had to go and live with him she would never have fallen in love with him. She just wished she'd told him so.

"So you see, that's why I couldn't let you get away. Even though it was a risk, I couldn't leave here until I knew you were dead. And now you will be." He stepped up beside the bed and rested one knee on it.

This was her chance.

He'd be overbalanced like that.

In one fluid motion, Ashley flung herself upward, shoving her hands into him, aiming for his solar plexus. She had no idea if she got him there or not, but she did manage to get him to stumble backward off the bed.

Ashley scrambled to her knees and climbed off on the opposite side to Evander. Her arms were tingling as regular blood flow resumed, but she brushed it off, she didn't have time for that right now.

She darted for the door.

Made it to it.

She flung it open and darted out into the hall.

There was no time to go to the kitchen and try to find a knife of her own. Her best bet was to run out into the street and hope that Evander followed and try to flag down help.

Unfortunately, she didn't make it that far.

She didn't even make it to the stairs.

Evander slammed into her, knocking her to the floor.

"You're a slippery one aren't you?" he said as he flipped her over onto her back. "I'm not taking any more chances with you."

The blade of the knife sliced through her neck.

~

2:48 P.M.

"We go in quiet," Sawyer said as Jett pulled the car to a stop in front of Ashley's house. "Killing Ash is his primary goal, and he's going to go for it even if he knows he's caught. One more murder isn't going to earn him any extra time in prison." With eighteen murders under his belt, plus the sexual assault and two counts of attempted murder of Ashley, Evander Hurley would already be spending the rest of his life in prison, assuming they got him alive. He had nothing to lose by killing Ashley, which meant they had nothing to bargain with.

"You three shouldn't even be going in," Morgan said. "You're not FBI agents, and you're not cops. You should be waiting in the car and let us handle this."

That was so ridiculous Sawyer didn't even bother replying. While he, Brady, and Michael may not be cops, both Brady and Michael had been before they left to work private security, and all three of them were trained and armed. They knew what they were doing, and they wouldn't mess this up.

Besides, Ashley was in there, and nothing was stopping him from going in.

"Maybe it would be better if you waited out here," Jett ventured cautiously.

Sawyer swung around to glare at his brother-in-law, angry at the betrayal, he'd thought that Jett out of everyone here would know how badly he needed to be a part of this.

"I'm Ashley's bodyguard," he hissed. He was, and he should never have let her come back here, even with the compromises she'd made, having Aurora and Samara with her, the security system, Brady spending the night, and getting a protection dog, none of those had done her any good. He should have insisted that if she couldn't stay with him then she needed to have another bodyguard on her at *all* times, not just Brady coming over later in the day. It had only been a few hours, and she hadn't been alone, they had all thought everything would be okay.

But they were wrong, and now Ashley was going to pay the price.

He should have known better.

He should have kept things professional.

He should have set his feelings for Ashley aside while it was his job to keep her safe.

"We're wasting time," Brady said, coming to his rescue, with Aurora in there he was just as panicked to get inside Ashley's house as Sawyer was.

"I don't want him getting away," Sawyer said. "Jett, you should stay out here, cover the front door, Morgan, you go round back, cover the back door."

"Why are we—the FBI agents—waiting outside while you three—the bodyguards—go inside?" Morgan asked.

"Is someone you love in that house?" Sawyer demanded.

"No." Morgan sighed, already knowing she was defeated.

"Then that's why."

Without any more discussion the five of them moved in on the house.

When he put his hand on the front door handle, Sawyer found the door unlocked, and had there been any doubt that Evander was here it evaporated. None of the women were stupid, there was no way they would leave the door unlocked whether they thought Evander would only come after Ashley when she was alone or not.

As he quietly eased the door the first thing Sawyer saw was blood.

A small puddle right by the door.

The second thing he saw was a pizza box and a woman's wallet lying on the floor by the door.

That was obviously how he had gotten in. The girls must have ordered pizza, Evander must have been watching the house, paid the delivery guy, and then rang the doorbell himself. The girls wouldn't have thought twice about opening the door when they were expecting someone to ring the bell. Evander had clearly been armed and had quickly injured whoever had opened the door, and then probably used them as a hostage to subdue the others.

Michael nudged his arm and gestured at the open basement door.

The house was quiet, and it was as good a place as any to start looking.

Quietly the three of them covered one another as they made their way to the door.

Sawyer was only halfway down the basement stairs when he saw them. Aurora and Samara were in the middle of the basement, one end of a string of Christmas lights tied around each of their necks. They were balancing on their tiptoes, and the string was pulled tight, it would only take one of them to lose balance, and the lights would tighten around the other's neck, strangling them.

There was no sign of Ashley.

Or Evander.

Brady was just a couple of steps behind him and must have seen them at the same time because he shoved past him and ran the rest of the way down into the basement.

Aurora and Samara obviously saw them as well because Aurora whispered, "Shh."

"Did he hurt you?" Brady demanded, wrapping an arm around his wife's waist and lifting her off the floor, easing the pressure around her neck.

"No," Aurora whispered.

"You're bleeding," Michael said to Samara as he also wrapped one arm around her waist and lifted her off the floor so the Christmas lights were no longer strangling either woman.

"I'm all right," Samara said, but her voice was weak and heavy with pain, and there was a large puddle of blood on the floor beneath her.

"I'll cut them down," Sawyer said, pulling a small Swiss army knife from his pocket and quickly cutting through the thin plastic of the string of lights.

As soon as he'd done so, Brady immediately began untangling the end from around his wife's neck, then once he had her free crushed her against him, kissing her like their lives depended on it. Michael did the same with Samara—minus the kissing—then ripped off his shirt and wrapped it around her bleeding arm.

"Where's Ashley?" Sawyer asked.

"Evander has her," Aurora replied. "He took her upstairs. He knows he has to be quick, you have to hurry."

He didn't need to be told twice.

"Get them out of here," he said to Brady and Michael, already heading for the stairs, at the bottom of which were piled several boxes of Christmas decorations. That must have been what they were doing down here before Evander showed up, getting all of Ashley's decorations out so they could decorate for tomorrow.

It was hard to believe that in just a few hours it would be Christmas Day.

Right now he needed a miracle to make sure Ashley survived to see it.

"We'll get them out and then come back," Brady said, but Sawyer wasn't really paying attention.

He was ready to go find the woman he loved. She might be angry with him, and he might have already lost her, but at least she'd be alive to yell at him.

Sawyer was halfway up the stairs when something somewhere in the house went bump.

Ashley and Evander.

"Stay down here," he called over his shoulder. If Evander was moving about up there he didn't want him stumbling upon them as they tried to leave. They were safer in the basement for the moment.

Taking the stairs three at a time, Sawyer reached the first floor, saw nothing, and headed for the second floor.

When he reached the top he saw Ashley lying in the hallway.

There was blood.

On her neck.

For a second the world seemed to stop spinning.

Was he too late?

Had Evander already killed Ashley?

On badly shaking legs he hurried toward her, dropping to his knees at her side.

Her eyes fluttered open, and he let out a sigh of relief.

She was alive.

The world could start spinning again.

"Ash," he murmured as he grabbed her scarf, which lay discarded on the floor beside her head. The wound on her neck was oozing blood, but it looked like it had missed the arteries. "Sorry," he said when she flinched as he pressed the scarf to the cut to stem the flow of blood. The bright red of the blood and the duller red of her scars fuelled his anger. Evander was going to pay for this.

Ashley smiled up at him. "You came, I knew you couldn't stay away."

"Not from you, my little snow obsessed best friend," he whispered back. Then he sobered. "Where's Evander?"

"I got out of the ropes he used to tie my hands behind my back and managed to get away. But I only got to here before he tackled me. He was going to slit my throat, but we heard your footsteps, and he ran."

When she talked it made her wound bleed more, and he already had what he needed from her, so Sawyer picked up one of her hands, angry to see the red marks encircling her wrists, and placed it on the handkerchief. "Hold this," he whispered. "Don't talk and don't move, I don't want you bleeding any more than you already are. Brady, Michael, Jett, and Morgan are here, he's not getting away this time."

Ashley's eyes grew wide, and she screamed, "Sawyer, behind you."

Instinct had him throwing his body down to cover hers, Evander was not taking the woman he loved from him.

Sharp, hot pain sliced through his back near his left shoulder as Evander plunged a knife into him.

All the injury did was stoke the fire already raging inside him.

This man had hurt Ashley.

For that he deserved to die a long, slow, agonizing death.

Right now though, Sawyer would settle for him just being dead.

He whirled around as Evander tried to come at him again and kicked out a foot, connecting with Evander's stomach and sending the man flying backward into the wall.

Evander was a tough one, and he didn't lose his hold on his weapon.

"You have until the count of three to drop the knife before I shoot you," Sawyer warned.

The other man just glared, a wild, manic look on his face as he realized he had been beaten and wasn't going to get to do what he'd come here to do.

"One."

Evander pushed away from the wall.

"Two."

Evander raised the knife above his head, ready to charge like a wounded bull who wasn't going down without a fight.

"Three."

Sawyer fired, shot Evander Hurley through the heart. The man's eyes grew round with surprise, the fierceness left them, and Sawyer could see once again the teenage boy who had been so horribly tortured by his peers.

As Evander's body dropped he stepped closer, kicked the knife away, then called over his shoulder, "We're clear up here, and Ashley needs an ambulance."

"I don't really," she said from behind him.

"What did I say about speaking?" Sawyer whirled around to find Ashley attempting to sit. He went back to her and knelt at her side, pressing her back to lie against the floorboards as he nudged her hand away and took over keeping pressure on her wound.

"I'm all right, Sawyer, really," she said.

"He could have killed you," he countered.

"But he didn't."

"An inch," he whispered. Now that Evander was dead the reality of what nearly happened was crashing down on him. An inch, one single inch, and he could have lost her. That was close. Too close. He was never leaving her side again, if she could forgive him.

"It's all right, it's over now," Ashley said, lifting her hand to cover his.

She was trying to console him, and she was the one who had almost died.

She was right though.

It was over.

Evander was dead, he was never going to kill again.

Sawyer just hoped that things weren't over between the two of them as well.

∼

7:13 P.M.

Ashley was back in the tree in Sawyer's yard.

It probably wasn't the smartest place to be sitting, considering she had three stitches in her neck and had been told by the paramedics to rest and take it easy.

She didn't want to sit inside though, she wanted to be out in the fresh air with the wind curling around her skin and tangling through her hair. She had been out here ever since the paramedics were done with them and Sawyer had brought her back to his place. She couldn't stay at her house since it was a crime scene, and she didn't really want to be there anyway.

The sky had been steadily filling with clouds, and Ashley hoped that meant it was finally going to snow. It would be Christmas Day in just a few hours and with the mess the last few months had been, and the even bigger mess the last few hours had been, she was already struggling to feel Christmassy, but without snow, it just wouldn't feel like Christmas at all.

"Hey."

She looked down to see Sawyer standing at the bottom of the tree with two mugs in his hands and a picnic blanket under one arm. "Hey," she said because she didn't really know what else to say. There were too many emotions and thoughts running around in her head, and she didn't know where to start. Ashley wasn't used to being nervous around Sawyer, but now there were so many butterflies in her stomach; it was like they had set up a whole planet in there. That was why it was such a risk to give in to her feelings for Sawyer, if they messed this up then she would always feel this way around him, and sooner rather than later, that was going to drive a wedge between them. A wedge she didn't think they could overcome.

But...

What if they didn't mess things up?

What if she and Sawyer worked as a couple just like they worked as best friends?

What if they could be happy together and have a future?

Didn't she owe it to both of them to at least give it a try?

"I made hot chocolate," Sawyer said, sounding as nervous as she felt. "You want to come down and have some?"

"Sure," she said. Her body was still stiff and sore from the fall down the hill at the park the other morning, and her neck ached with a dull ripping kind of pain every time she moved her head, so climbing down the tree was awkward.

Sawyer set the mugs down and reached up to help her down the last bit then hesitated. "You want some help?"

"Thanks," she said. This awkwardness between them had to stop, they had to talk, now. Sawyer's hands wrapped around her waist and lifted her down, then he picked up her mug and passed it to her. Ashley smiled when she saw what was sitting in the hot chocolate. "You made the marshmallow snowmen."

"The same ones you made this morning."

This morning.

Was it really only twelve hours or so since she and Sawyer had planned to spend the day watching Christmas movies? Since she had found the pearls in Sawyer's jacket pocket and learned of his feelings for her?

It felt like that was months ago.

"Hold this," he said as he held out his mug. Ashley took it, and Sawyer spread the blanket out on the grass, then she gave him back his mug, and they both sat down.

For a few minutes the two of them just sat in companionable silence. The awkwardness was still there, but regardless it was nice just to sit side by side, sipping hot chocolate, under the cloudy sky, enjoying the quiet. It was nice knowing that there was no longer someone walking the planet who wanted her dead. It made her feel peaceful, a different kind of peace, an inner peace, like her equilibrium had been restored.

"How's your neck?" Sawyer asked. "Do you need more painkillers?"

"No, it's okay for now. How's your shoulder?" She wasn't the only one the paramedics had attended to back at her house. Sawyer had gotten three stitches in the knife wound on his back, and Samara had beaten them both and needed a total of nine stitches to close the deep wound in her arm. Luckily stitches were all they had needed and not body bags, the only one to leave the house in one was Evander, and that made the world a safer place for everyone.

"I can take you back to your house if you want, crime scene is finished there, and it's been cleaned," Sawyer said, breaking the silence.

"No, I don't want to go back there." Possibly ever, but she wasn't worrying about that right now. "Even though all I've wanted for the last nearly four months was to go back home, once I got there it felt different. It didn't feel like home anymore because..." Ashley trailed off, embarrassed to finish that sentence. How could she expect Sawyer to open up his home to her permanently just because it now felt like her home too? Especially with their complicated relationship, even if they were going to be a couple that didn't mean she could just move in here.

"Because here feels like home now?" Sawyer asked hopefully.

"Yes," she answered simply. There was no point in lying. If they were going to try dating then they had to be honest with each other, no more lies.

"So, does this mean that you don't hate me?"

"Oh, Sawyer, I never hated you. I was shocked and angry to find out you lied to me, and at first I did feel like you took advantage of the situation, but I know you, and I know you would never do that."

"You really never knew?" Sawyer asked.

"I really didn't. I thought we were just friends, best friends. I never looked at you that way until just a few days ago. We've been spending even more time together than we used to, and you were so supportive, and I realized that I felt something for you, something beyond friendship. That scared me. I was afraid of losing the only stable thing in my life. I was afraid of losing you."

"You would never lose me." Sawyer reached over and took her hand.

"I know, but I was scared that if we dated and things didn't work out for some reason, then we couldn't hang out like this anymore, and I would rather have had you as a friend and deal with the feelings I was developing than risk anything ruining what we have. But then, when I was at my house I realized that I had lost you anyway. Aurora, Samara, and I talked, and they made me remember that you have to face your fears, and that I promised my mom when she was dying that I would never have regrets. Were you ever going to tell me?" Ashley asked. If she hadn't found the pearls she knew he wouldn't have told her now, but she wondered if he would ever have confessed.

"I honestly don't know, Ash. I tried telling you, and you fell asleep. I tried again, but you seemed so upset that anything would ruin our friendship that I backed out and decided I wouldn't ever say anything. Something might have changed at some point, but I was scared too because of everything you just said. It's scary to put our friendship on the line to see if there could be something else there."

"But that's what we're going to do, right?" She could feel Sawyer's eyes on her even if she couldn't see more than the shadowy outline of his face.

"I'm game if you are."

"I'm game," she said quickly. She could feel goosebumps breaking out all over her skin that had nothing to do with the cold night. Those butterflies were back in her stomach, and this time it wasn't because she was anxious about what was going to happen with Sawyer, this time it was because she wanted to kiss him. "You know the last few days I didn't just realize that I like you as more than a friend."

"Oh?" Sawyer said, his voice husky.

"You know when we were in the bath the other day, playing with the fake snow?"

"Yeah."

"And when you were cleaning the blood off my face after I fell at the park?"

"Yes."

"I wanted to kiss you."

"We were interrupted both times."

"There's no one here to interrupt us tonight," Ashley said, her breath catching in nervous anticipation. What was it like to kiss your best friend? She had only been intimate with a couple of guys because she wanted to wait for the right guy before she made things too serious.

Sawyer could be the right guy.

They made each other laugh, had fun together, knew each other's fears and joys, they understood each other, the foundation for an amazing relationship had already been laid.

Kissing him had to be better than kissing anyone else because what she felt for him was real and deep.

She wasn't just developing feelings for him, she was in love with him.

Sawyer's hand curled around the back of her neck, carefully avoiding the white, square bandage taped over the gash, and drew her closer, dipping his head to meet hers. And then finally, his lips were touching her own, softly, sweetly, experimentally, then deeper and more passionately as they both felt the click of the other piece of their soul snapping into place.

Sometimes you found love when you weren't even looking for it.

Friends to lovers, they were meant to be.

~

8:06 P.M.

"You know," Ashley said slowly, breathlessly, when they finally broke the kiss, "kissing you wasn't the only thing I wanted to do with you. The other night when you slept in my bed with me after I had a nightmare, and you were walking around all half-naked, I wanted to do a whole lot more than just kiss."

"Oh really," Sawyer wriggled his eyebrows even though he knew she couldn't see him very well in the dark.

"Yes, really." She giggled, sounding so carefree and relaxed, so happy. Her happiness was the best Christmas gift he could ask for.

As much as he would love to have Ashley naked in his bed, given that Evander Hurley had slashed her neck, he didn't think that sex was what the paramedics had in mind when they told her to go home and go to bed.

"Maybe we should wait a few days until you're better," he said, pointing at her neck.

"Hey, you're the one with the hole in his back," she retorted.

Sawyer kept forgetting about the knife wound in his back. It didn't hurt, he was sure the pain would come, but right now he was riding a high knowing Ashley was alive and no longer in danger. And now that he and Ashley had talked things through and he knew she wasn't angry with him and that they were both prepared to take the risk and try dating, his wound was the last thing on his mind.

Especially since he knew the two of them dating wasn't a risk.

When they'd kissed he'd felt it, and he knew Ashley had too. They were meant to be together. They were in love. They might not have actually said the words, but it was what it was.

"We're both going to be sore tomorrow, but that's tomorrow, tonight is tonight, and it's Christmas Eve, we deserve this," Ashley wheedled, wiggling closer so she was basically in his lap.

As though she sensed he was very nearly convinced and just needed one more tiny little push, she scrambled up onto her knees and whispered her lips softly across his.

Very softly.

Tantalizingly softly.

"If I see any blood on your neck I'm taking you to the hospital to spend the night," he warned.

Even though there was only the dim light shining through the kitchen windows to light the yard, he could see Ashley make a face at that, but she nodded. "Deal."

Sawyer wrapped his arms around her waist and stood, taking her up with him. Ashley wrapped her legs around his waist and nibbled on his ear as he carried her inside.

"Ash," he moaned.

"Sorry," she said, sounding cheerfully unsorry.

He loved that they could tease each other like this, they already knew each other so well, and knowing that his feelings for her were reciprocated was the best feeling on the planet. For so long he had believed that there was no chance, that he was destined to spend the rest of his life stuck in the unrequited love basket, and now he had the only thing he wanted this Christmas.

"Two can play that game," he told her. Keeping hold of her with one arm, his other hand slid up under the hem of her sweater and brushed very lightly along the underside of her breasts.

"Sawyer," she whined when he withdrew his hand.

"Don't like it when the shoe's on the other foot, huh?" He smirked.

Ashley laughed. "I was worried things would be awkward with this, you know seeing each other naked, and having sex and stuff, because we've been friends for so long, but it's not, it just feels so natural. Because of you, because you're so amazing, I just love you."

He froze halfway up the stairs.

Her mouth dropped open as she realized what she'd just said.

"Oh," she said, embarrassed. "Maybe it's too soon to say that. I mean, I, uh, I know you said this morning that you, ah, um..."

He crushed his mouth to hers.

He'd known that she had feelings for him and wanted them to date, but he hadn't known for sure that she actually loved him the way he loved her.

And now he did.

This day couldn't get any more perfect.

It had gone from the worst day of his life to the best in just the space of a few hours.

"That was okay to say?" Ashley asked when he ended the kiss.

"Do you mean it?"

"Yes," she answered without hesitation. "I've known it for a few days now."

"Then it was the most perfect thing you could ever have said."

He carried her up the rest of the way to the bedroom and laid her out on the bed. As much as he wanted her naked there was something else he wanted first.

"Ash?" he asked, brushing a stray lock of hair off her cheek.

"Yeah?"

"Your scarf," he said, trailing his fingers down her cheek and chin and stopping them just above the edge of the scarf. The first thing she'd done after Evander was dead and she knew the paramedics were coming was to ask him to get another scarf for her from her room. "Can we take it off?"

Panic briefly flitted through her eyes, but then it faded. "I guess you already saw the scars earlier today anyway."

"You know I don't care about them, right?"

"I know." She smiled and reached up to undo the scarf, letting it slide through her fingers and flutter down to the mattress.

Sawyer wasn't quite sure that she did.

To prove it to her, he touched his lips to her neck, kissing every inch of it. Then he trailed a line of kisses down her chest, unzipping her sweater as he went. She wasn't wearing a bra, and he touched the lightest of kisses to her nipples, causing Ashley to groan in impatient frustration, her chest lifting off the mattress.

"Patience, patience." He laughed. He pulled her sweatpants and underwear along with them, down her legs and tossed them on the floor, his own clothes joined hers.

When he looked back up he saw that Ashley had tensed. Gone was the lustful excitement, her flushed cheeks had paled, and her fingers had curled into the sheets.

She'd told him about her worries that being raped shouldn't affect her because she didn't remember it.

That was ridiculous and couldn't be less true.

Of course being raped was going to affect you regardless of whether you remembered the actual event or not.

"Sweetheart, if you don't want to that's okay." He knelt beside her and brushed his knuckles across her forehead.

"No, I do want to, it's just I haven't since...and what if I freak out?" She looked up at him anxiously.

"Then we stop, or we keep going, or whatever you want to do. It's fine, honey, whatever you can deal with we do, or don't do. You know that I love you, you're safe here, you don't have to be embarrassed or worried, you know I'm not interested in you for sex, and I've waited this long, I can wait longer, I can wait for you forever."

His words seemed to smooth away some of her fears and Ashley relaxed again. "I don't want to wait."

"Okay, you tell me if you change your mind," he told her. Since he knew kissing didn't seem to stress her out, he went back to that, and when he felt the tension flow out of her body, he let his hands start to slowly roam her body, she stiffened when his hands first started moving, but when he slowed it down even more she quickly relaxed.

He touched every inch of her, memorized every sound she made, what she liked, and what didn't do anything for her. Sawyer enjoyed every second of exploring her and when his hand finally found its way between her legs he found her wet and more than ready for him. He teased her for a while, working her closer to release and making sure that she was ready for it.

"I love you, Ash," he said as he slowly eased into her. He was prepared for her to have the freak out she was worried about, but when their eyes met he saw she was in the zone.

"I love you, too," she said.

Together they moved, their bodies in perfect harmony, working each other higher and higher. Sawyer could feel himself getting close, but he didn't want to come until Ashley did. He didn't have to wait long, a moment later she came with a scream and a contented moan, and he came seconds after with a scream and a contented moan of his own.

"That was amazing," Ashley sighed.

"It was," Sawyer agreed, pulling out of her and stretching out at her side so he could spoon her against him.

"So that's what sex with the person you love is like, huh?"

"Pretty perfect," he said, snuggling her closer. "You want to stay in bed, get some sleep? If you're hungry I can make you some dinner first."

"I'm not really hungry, and I'm not tired, I'm too wired to sleep. Tomorrow is Christmas, and even though it's been a rough holiday season this year now I'm excited. Evander is dead, I have you, I'm finally getting my Christmas spirit, I want to do something Christmassy." Ashley was vibrating with excitement.

"Then I have the perfect idea, I suspected you might feel like this, so I asked Michael to bring the boxes with your Christmas decorations over here. You want to go decorate your Christmas tree?"

Ashley squealed with delight and spun around in his arms to plant a kiss on his lips. "I love that you know me so well. Let's go do that."

"I know you said you weren't hungry, but Savannah dropped off some Christmas goodies," Sawyer told her as he released his hold on Ashley and reached for their clothes.

"I love Savannah's baking, I love your sister, I love you, I love everything right now." Ashley grinned. "It's Christmas." She shrugged when she saw him watching her with an amused smile.

"You want your scarf?" he asked, holding it out.

She reached for it, took it, staring at it for a long moment, then she let it go, watching it fluttering to the floor. "I don't need it."

This woman couldn't get more amazing.

She had been raped and almost murdered three times, she had lived close to four months with the threat of a killer hunting her, she had fought back today when Evander had come after her, and now she was taking the first steps in letting go and moving on.

Sawyer had never known it was possible to love someone like he loved Ashley.

He was the luckiest guy alive.

CHAPTER
Seven

December 25th
7:44 A.M.

"No, I think that should go over there," Ashley said when Sawyer put a snowman decoration on the tree. They'd been decorating all night.

Well, *almost* all night.

They'd pigged out on an array of baked treats Savannah had left for them, they'd sipped hot chocolate in front of the roaring fireplace, and they'd had another two rounds of lovemaking. Each time it got a little easier and her fears that she would embarrass herself by having a panic attack faded. She didn't have to worry about that with Sawyer. Even if it did happen there would be nothing to be embarrassed about. Sawyer would never make her feel self-conscious about anything.

"Where do you want it then?" he asked.

Ashley took a step back to survey the tree, it was almost done, and there wasn't a lot of space left for the rest of the decorations. "Hmm, maybe there," she said, pointing to a spot down near the bottom.

"Here?" Sawyer asked, adding the decoration.

"Perfect." She nodded.

"There's only five more. Five more *snowmen*," he added. "Why am I not surprised almost all your decorations are snowmen? I think you have even more than you did last year."

"I *may* have gone shopping in the after Christmas sales to buy some." She giggled. "You can never have too many snowmen." She just wished she could go outside and build a real snowman. Despite the clouds that had built up last night there was still no snow. She should know, she had been checking every hour on the hour, going out into the yard just to make sure there were not snow flurries she couldn't see from the window.

"We're going to have to put you on a snowman diet." Sawyer rolled his eyes at her.

"Okay, and you can go on a sports team's diet," she shot back.

"Touché." He smirked.

Ashley rolled her eyes back at Sawyer. "Let's just put the last few decorations on, then we can have breakfast. Let's make French toast."

"Then we should maybe grab a couple of hours sleep. If you like we can try to make it to Savannah's for dinner."

"Definitely." She couldn't wait to celebrate Christmas with friends.

She and Sawyer added the last couple of decorations, then they both stepped back and admired their handiwork. The tree was beautiful. Stunning really, she loved it.

"Time to put the angel on top," she announced, picking up her very favorite decoration. It was actually a gift from Sawyer the first Christmas after they met. It was a snowman angel, and it was so pretty, it was white and shimmery, with fluffy white feathers for wings. "You can't complain about this snowman, you're the one who got it for me," she said as she passed it to him. "Can you put it on for me?"

Sawyer reached up and set the snowman angel right on top of the tree.

Now it was finished, and everything looked just perfect. The tinsel sparkled, the decorations added splashes of color against the green of the tree, and the tinsel's silver and gold.

"Want me to turn the lights on?" Sawyer asked.

Ashley couldn't stop a small shudder rolling through her. She really never was going to look at Christmas lights the same way again. As amazing as last night had been, and as determined as she was to keep her focus on the future not the past, she knew she was always going to be affected by what Evander Hurley had done to her. There would never be a time where it went away, but she could make sure that she didn't make it her focus. With time and help she knew she'd get there.

"You okay?" Sawyer slipped an arm around her shoulder and kissed her temple.

"Yeah, just thinking," she said, leaning into him.

"You have time, Ash. It isn't a race, take your time, and you'll eventually get to where you want to be."

"And I have you to help me which makes it so much less scary." She was so lucky to have her best friend as her boyfriend. What could be better? Now she got to be with her best friend every day forever.

"Were you serious when you said that my house feels like your home now?" he asked, his fingers combing through her hair that was hanging loose around her shoulders.

"Yes. I love it here, it feels like my home because it's *your* home, because you're here." She knew it was too soon to hope Sawyer might ask her to move in, but it was going to be hard when she had to go back to her house.

"Move in with me?" Sawyer asked as though he'd just read her mind.

"Isn't it too soon? Are you sure? Are you serious?" She fired off questions, trying not to sound too desperate but knowing she was failing.

"Were you serious about getting a dog?" Sawyer asked.

"I don't know what the right answer to that is." She laughed because she knew he was just teasing her. "But, yeah, I kind of like the idea of getting a dog."

"That was the right answer. I've wanted to get a dog for a while now but just never got around to it. Seriously though, Ash." He turned her around to face him and took her hands. "I'd love to have you move in here with me."

"Then I accept." Maybe this was moving fast, but really they had known each other for three years, they were best friends who knew everything about each other—or at least they did now that Sawyer's big secret was out—they had been living together for the last nearly four months, and they were in love.

Sawyer kissed her, and she got that great feeling all through her body that happened every time their lips touched.

She was going to say they should go back up to bed when her eyes fell on something outside.

"Sawyer," she shrieked way too loudly. "It's snowing."

Ashley didn't wait to hear his response, she ran to the back door, threw on her coat and boots, and ran out into the yard. The snow was coming down quick and fast, and she threw her arms out wide, tilted her head back, and let the snow fall upon her.

This was just what she wanted, snow for Christmas.

Now everything was perfect.

Actually perfect.

She couldn't have asked for anything more even if she had a genie in a bottle and three wishes.

She dropped down into the snow and made a snow angel, then bounced back up and began to spin in circles in time with the fluttering snowflakes.

"You're such a goofball." Sawyer laughed from where he was standing, rugged up, leaning against the side of the house.

Ashley didn't care, she was too happy to sit inside. It was snowing, and she was in love with Sawyer, and it was Christmas morning.

"Let's make a snowman," she said as she dropped down to her knees and began to grab handfuls of snow with her bare hands, she'd be cold later, but right now, she didn't care.

"Aren't you freezing?" Sawyer asked as he came to help.

"Nope," she sang happily. "You do the body, I'll do the head."

Sawyer rolled the small snowball until it grew bigger and bigger, collecting the fresh white snow to make a three-foot round snowman body. She made her own ball, smaller than Sawyer's, and lifted it to set it on top.

"Now we need a carrot for the nose and something for the mouth," she announced.

"Here you go." Sawyer pulled a carrot and several lumps of coal from his pocket.

"Where did you get the coal?"

"I bought it weeks ago, hoping you'd get your snow for Christmas."

"You really are the best," she said happily as she used the carrot and coal to give her snowman a face. While Sawyer wasn't looking, she quickly bent down and grabbed a handful of snow, forming it into a snowball as she stood, then spinning around and tossing it at Sawyer.

Sawyer spluttered as the snow exploded in his face, then threw back his head and laughed. "Why, you little, snow-loving monster. I'm going to get you for that one."

Ashley shrieked and took off across the yard, Sawyer on her heels. He caught her easily and threw her to the ground, holding the back of her head as he did so to cushion the blow and not break her stitches.

With a smile she couldn't wipe off her face even if she tried, her eyes met Sawyer's and she saw the love shining from his. Ashley wondered how she had never seen it before. Maybe it was because the timing hadn't been right, she hadn't been in the same place he was.

But now she was.

And now they could start their lives together.

"Merry Christmas, Ash."

"Merry Christmas, Sawyer. Now kiss me."

They're both battling demons from their pasts, can they find a way to look to the future instead? Find out in the next book in this thrilling romantic suspense series!

Yuletide Guard (Christmas Romantic Suspense #5)

Also by Jane Blythe

Detective Parker Bell Series

A SECRET TO THE GRAVE
WINTER WONDERLAND
DEAD OR ALIVE
LITTLE GIRL LOST
FORGOTTEN

Count to Ten Series

ONE
TWO
THREE
FOUR
FIVE
SIX
BURNING SECRETS
SEVEN
EIGHT
NINE
TEN

Broken Gems Series

CRACKED SAPPHIRE

CRUSHED RUBY

FRACTURED DIAMOND

SHATTERED AMETHYST

SPLINTERED EMERALD

SALVAGING MARIGOLD

River's End Rescues Series

COCKY SAVIOR

SOME REGRETS ARE FOREVER

SOME FEARS CAN CONTROL YOU

SOME LIES WILL HAUNT YOU

SOME QUESTIONS HAVE NO ANSWERS

SOME TRUTH CAN BE DISTORTED

SOME TRUST CAN BE REBUILT

SOME MISTAKES ARE UNFORGIVABLE

Candella Sisters' Heroes Series

LITTLE DOLLS

LITTLE HEARTS

LITTLE BALLERINA

Storybook Murders Series

NURSERY RHYME KILLER

FAIRYTALE KILLER

FABLE KILLER

Saving SEALs Series

SAVING RYDER
SAVING ERIC
SAVING OWEN
SAVING LOGAN
SAVING GRAYSON
SAVING CHARLIE

Prey Security Series

PROTECTING EAGLE
PROTECTING RAVEN
PROTECTING FALCON
PROTECTING SPARROW
PROTECTING HAWK
PROTECTING DOVE

Prey Security: Alpha Team Series

DEADLY RISK
LETHAL RISK
EXTREME RISK
FATAL RISK
COVERT RISK
SAVAGE RISK

Prey Security: Artemis Team Series

About the Author

USA Today bestselling author Jane Blythe writes action-packed romantic suspense and military romance featuring protective heroes and heroines who are survivors. One of Jane's most popular series includes Prey Security, part of Susan Stoker's OPERATION ALPHA world! Writing in that world alongside authors such as Janie Crouch and Riley Edwards has been a blast, and she looks forward to bringing more books to this genre, both within and outside of Stoker's world. When Jane isn't binge-reading she's counting down to Christmas and adding to her 200+ teddy bear collection!

To connect and keep up to date please visit any of the following